MINE

AN
ANTHOLOGY
OF BODY
AUTONOMY
HORROR

MINE

AN
ANTHOLOGY
OF BODY
AUTONOMY
HORROR

EDITED BY
ROXIE VOORHEES
& NICO BELL

Creature Publishing
Brooklyn, NY

ISBN 9781951971113
LCCN 2022948636

Cover design by Luísa Dias
Spine illustration by Rachel Kelli

CREATUREHORROR.COM

🐦 @creaturelit

📷 @creaturepublishing

To *every* person

TABLE OF CONTENTS

Dear Readers,

On June 24, 2022, the United States Supreme Court overturned Roe v. Wade deeming it illegal for womb-owners across the nation to make reproductive health care decisions for themselves. From the justified outrage came a deep desire to fight back. This sparked *Mine: An Anthology of Body Horror* with the intention to showcase the terrors associated when body autonomy is denied. The profits from this anthology will go to National Abortion Rights Action League (NARAL) which is an organization dedicated to fighting for reproductive freedom, access to birth control and abortion care, paid parental leave, birth control, and protection from pregnancy discrimination.

Please note that trigger warnings are provided at the end of this collection.

Nico Bell and *Roxie Voorhees*

WOMB
Kelly Brocklehurst

They imagined: sticking needles deep
into all the places it hurt, popping
their uterus like a balloon;

blood gushing from their vagina, a hot
and welcome relief, sullying the toilet
so red they'd have to replace it later;

the fibroid blocking blood from getting
out, their uterus filling until it burst.
They breathed as if in labor, their cramps

contractions that didn't push anything out.
Their gynecologist had denied
performing a hysterectomy, saying,

You might change your mind.
They didn't have needles, but their reflection
in the thin, curved blade of the knife said

it would do just fine. They plunged it into soft
skin as far as they could, the blade sliding
past fat and muscle, trying to find what made

them feel as though they were dying. Their abdomen
pulsed, and they cradled their hands gently
together as their uterus, small and red, slipped out.

PRE-BABY BODIES
Anne Gresham

Birth changes you.

Take me, for example. I was apparently now the kind of person who dragged herself into a 5 a.m. barre class—that's how desperate I was to feel like I belonged in my own body again.

"Hi!" the instructor Jenna chirped. Her: a lithe twenty-something with a blond ponytail whose bounce and volume belonged on the back end of an animated unicorn, clad in a shimmery pink tank, coordinating lavender sports bra, and heather leggings. Me: three months postpartum, hoping against hope my double-bagged boobs didn't leak all over the studio, rocking a faded T-shirt from a staff retreat six years ago and the pair of sweatpants I'd basically been living in and occasionally peeing on ever since Micah was born. At least I'd washed them.

I had, right? Shit.

"You must be new," Jenna continued. "The hardest part is showing up! The girls'll show you what you need." Her

5

assessment of my physical condition was fast, but I didn't miss it. "Anything I should know before we get started?"

"Oh. Um. Yeah," I stammered. "I . . . I just had a baby and I'm just, um, having trouble feeling like myself again. Does that make sense?"

How do you explain the Humpty Dumpty-style disorientation of postpartum recovery? I was still me, but not. The same store, but all the clothes were on the wrong hangers. The same set of watercolors, but the paints were so mixed up they were all the same shade of muddy brown.

Jenna smiled beatifically. "Absolutely. You want your pre-baby body back! You're in the right place!"

Am I? I wondered, looking around. On what planet was this the right place for me? The studio was lovely, with large windows looking out over a ravine, barely visible in the predawn darkness. The class was full, but in spite of the brutal hour, they all seemed so awake, relaxed, and comfortable. Everyone seemed genuinely happy to see each other, and they wore their belonging as casually as their grippy socks and scrunchies. Worse, the majority had bodies that looked like they'd already been doing this workout every day of their genetically blessed lives.

I felt so shamefully, desperately jealous of them.

I'd been a runner before Micah. I wasn't particularly fast or competitive, but I'd run a half marathon and could happily jog five miles before brunch. I'd also done a little powerlifting; again, nothing extreme, but I had worked up to a 200-pound deadlift. Even if I wasn't an athlete, I'd been in shape and comfortable moving through the world wrapped in my own ratio of skin, blood, fat, and muscle.

But then, Micah. Micah, with his sudden fetal growth spurts and an attendant bout of preeclampsia that landed me on bedrest. Micah, who came barreling out of me like a cannonball. Micah, whose placenta left behind an internal wound the size of a paper plate. A fast, easy birth! A fuckton of unmentionably placed stitches!

And so here I was, feeling like a half-rotted jack-o'-lantern, nursing around the clock, back at work full time, waiting for a 5 a.m. barre class to start in a frantic bid to put myself back together.

"Hey!" a friendly voice said. "New?"

I turned around and nodded sheepishly. The kind-eyed woman behind me was short, friendly, and looked to be in her late thirties or early forties.

"I'm Lily," she said.

"Meg," I replied, feeling unaccountably shy.

She grinned. "Don't be intimidated by all this. It's easier when you know what to expect."

"They said that about birth, too," I blurted, and then immediately worried it was a weird overshare.

But Lily snorted. "No shit," she agreed. "Mine was born eight months ago, and I'm only just now feeling like a person again."

"But you do feel like a person again eventually?" I snatched at the life preserver she had just tossed in my direction. "Mine's three months old, and I don't know how I can keep going like this."

She squeezed my shoulder. "You'd be amazed how much easier it gets when you can get six hours of sleep a night. I swear. Come on, let's get your stuff."

Lily helped me pick out a resistance band, a mat, a squishy ball, and a set of hand weights. I reached for the larger size, but she stopped me. "Do the half pounders," she said. "Trust me."

I thought mournfully of that 200-pound deadlift but followed her advice.

Then Jenna turned on the music, and the room was overwhelmed with extremely loud gym pop. Jenna bounded to the front like a gazelle, her overwhelming energy preemptively wearing me out.

"Jenna's sweet," Lily said, "but she's a beast. Good luck!"

"Okay ladies!" Jenna bellowed like a Valkyrie. "Let's DO this!"

And then she proceeded to absolutely kick my ass, one "down an inch, up an inch" at a time.

When class ended at 6:15, my hamstrings were on fire and my core was quivering jelly, but I actually felt better than I had in months.

"You were awesome!" Lily said as we put up our mats. "You gonna try again, you think?"

"Yeah, maybe," I said.

"Here, let me give you my number," she said and pulled out her phone. "Moms. We've gotta stick together, right?"

"Yeah," I grinned. My eyes started watering, and I hoped she couldn't see. I'd heard about the importance of mom friends, had absolutely zero, and now one had apparently fallen into my lap.

We walked out to the still-dark parking lot together, swapping baby photos on our phones.

"Thanks," I told her. "Seriously. It was great to meet you. Maybe I'll see you here again?"

"For sure. I'm here every Monday, Wednesday, and Friday."

"Excuse me," said a new voice. We turned to find a slender ballet-bodied woman with an ageless face and shark-like eyes.

"I just wanted you to know," she purred. "We have a special class for new mothers, free of charge. It meets on Thursdays at midnight."

"Mid—midnight?" I spluttered.

The woman nodded. "We've found it works out well for people who have to sneak in workouts between night feedings. Here, take a reminder card. We'd love to see you."

There was something badly off about her, but I took the card anyway. "Thanks," I said.

Lily raised her eyebrows as the woman walked away. "Midnight?" She whistled. "Jesus. I mean, if that's the only time you can make a barre class, maybe it's just not the season for that?"

I shrugged. The rational part of me knew that Lily was right, but another part of me saw the logic. Really, 11 p.m. to 2 a.m. was my most reliable chance not to have to nurse. It was when I read, and googled, and worried. Maybe trying to get back into shape wouldn't be the worst use of that time, since I was currently squandering it every night.

But this morning, at least, I was leaving with another mom's phone number, and that made everything feel a little less heavy.

❖ ❖ ❖

The temporary endorphin rush of the workout dissolved as soon as I got home.

Micah was *screaming*. When a baby cries like that, you'll do anything, anything at all, to make it stop.

But I could also hear another sound: the deeper, vibrating ebb and flow of Josh snoring.

"Motherfucker!" I shrieked in Josh's direction and ran into Micah's room.

His tiny little head looked like a furious tomato. How long had he been crying like this? I whipped out a sweaty boob, but the poor little guy's gale-force howling was so strong he couldn't latch. All he could do was snap futilely at my poor sore nipple.

"I'm sorry," I yelled over the sound of him screaming. "I'm so sorry, I'm so sorry." My own tears started then, along with my letdown, which was so hard and heavy there was no way the kid could handle it, even if he had been able to catch his breath.

"Please!" I sobbed at Micah. "Please, stop, I'm so sorry."

I wasn't cut out for this. Why the fuck did I think it was a good idea for me—selfish, easily discouraged me—to be someone's mother? The future flashed before my eyes of failure after parental failure, ending in Micah working with his therapist to outline the terms of his long-overdue estrangement from me.

Josh stumbled into Micah's room and stared bemusedly at the wailing pair of us. "Y'all okay?" he asked groggily.

"No!" I yelled. "No, *Josh,* we're not. Where the fuck were you?"

Josh's big brown eyes were confused and hurt. "Calm down," he muttered and puttered off to brush his teeth and enjoy his morning bowel movement and phone time, which I've clocked at upwards of twenty minutes.

I did calm down because there was no choice. And Micah did too because he only had so much energy. Eventually, I got him latched and guzzling pitifully. Then after Josh made his way out the door, into his empty car where he listened to music in peace and sipped coffee I made for him all the way to work, I juggled Micah through my own morning routine, gathered up his daycare supplies, and bundled him into my backseat.

When I sat down behind the wheel, the exhaustion settled in like a thick fog. I shouldn't have gone to that class. There was no way I was going to be able to make it through the day.

❖❖❖

Daycare drop off. Late for work. Stare at my inbox. Poke at a spreadsheet. Pump. Cry. Delete a few emails. Lunch. Donuts in the breakroom, thank fuck.

"Still eating for two, huh?" my manager joked. I hated myself for laughing instead of reporting his ass immediately to HR.

Pump. Snap paper clips. Continue to fail to catch up on email. Design custom vinyl labels for sippy cups, which maybe we'll need soon. Get caught. Feel like a terrible employee. A worse mother.

Pump. Cry.

Coat. Keys. Milk. Car. Gas, break, and I'm. Just. So. Tired. I can't—

A car horn blared behind me and I snapped awake. The light had changed. I stomped on the accelerator and turned left. More horns shrieked. Why was that car so close? Oh God, did I not have the right-of-way? Oh my God, I have to fix this. I have to do something. Anything.

Daycare pickup. Crying kids, including mine. I'm not bringing enough milk. He's not napping well.

Home. Nurse. Laundry. Dinner. Nurse. Put Micah down. Pick him up. Back down. Back up.

Cry.

❖❖❖

Josh wandered through the living room where I was clutching Micah to my chest, tears streaming down my face.

"What's with you?" he asked after a minute.

I blinked.

"It's like you're not even trying." He shook his head and wandered out.

I looked at myself in the black mirror of the TV, and I could see my flabby body, my stringy hair. I didn't know who I hated more, Josh or me.

Later, while nursing Micah, I started tapping out my sad, lonely rosary into Google.

Not liking motherhood
Not good at motherhood
Hate the way I look
How to fix body after childbirth
How to fix body when I hate it
How to not hate my body
How to not hate myself

Everything I read suggested exercise. *But I tried that*, I wanted to plead with the internet. I swear, I did. It was supposed to lift my mood, tone my blasted belly, improve my milk supply, give me confidence. But I tried exercise and still came home to a total shitshow. Apparently, I couldn't have an hour and a half to myself anymore.

Unless.

There was that midnight class. I could still try that.

❖ ❖ ❖

But I didn't want to go alone. I felt awkward, but I texted Lily and tried to talk her into going with me. She, like a reasonable adult, did her best to talk me out of it.

<Can I call you really fast? Is that weird?>

That text hit me in a really surprisingly soft spot. I had college friends, and work friends, but not call-me friends. I hadn't talked to anyone on the phone besides my own mom since Micah was born.

<Sure> I responded, like this was normal for me, even though I was a little worried I was going to burst into tears.

My phone buzzed, and I answered.

"Hey," I said, doing my level best to sound like a normal person.

"Hey!" she answered. "Listen, I just wanted to be sure you were okay."

"Huh?"

I heard her sigh. "I mean, I'm so sorry if I'm being an asshole and overstepping, it's just, it's really hard at first. Like, really hard. And you seemed like you might be struggling."

I swallowed. I didn't remember saying anything particularly *off* at barre. Like mentioning the possible merits of crossing death off my to-do list now to save myself several decades of unnecessary worry.

"I don't know," I answered, surprised by my own honesty. "Yes, I mean. No. I don't know. It is really, really hard."

"Seriously, you're still in that postpartum haze. Maybe don't kill yourself trying to roll back the clock right now, okay? I'm telling you, a daily walk in the sunshine counts. And some days even managing that can be too much."

I knew she was right. But I didn't know if I could stand being in this body, and in this brain, without doing everything I could to change it.

"I know," I said. "I just don't know what else to do."

"Maybe instead of going to this midnight barre class—I mean, you hear how wacky that sounds right? But maybe instead, if you wanted to, you could come over. Bring your kiddo. Let me make you dinner. Swear I'm not a serial killer."

"That's exactly what a serial killer would say."

She laughed.

I wish I'd said yes. I wish I'd gone to her house, eaten at her table, met her family. I wanted to. But I caught a glimpse of myself in the mirror. It wasn't really even the weight that repulsed me. That was fine—I've always been big and I've never minded my curves. It was the horrible feeling of looking at myself and not recognizing my own haggard reflection, of seeing this sad, exhausted, unloveable, unfuckable creature so at odds with who I thought I was.

So I doubled down.

"Come on," I said, trying to sound casual. "It'll be fun. Give it a try with me? Then I'll take you up on dinner some other time."

"Okay," she said after a beat. "To be clear, I think this is a horrible idea. But only on the condition that you really do take me up on something normal. You have to do something fun for yourself, too."

I will always wonder how things would have turned out if I'd just listened to her.

❖ ❖ ❖

"I cannot believe you talked me into this," Lily grumbled when we met in front of the studio. The lot was dark except for one sputtering streetlight, and the night silent except for the occasional rustle of the leaves in the lot behind the studio and the occasional woosh of a car down the nearby interstate.

"How is this any more outlandish than 5 a.m.?" I countered.

"Is there even anyone here? All the lights are off."

I frowned at the dark building. But then I saw movement inside. "Someone's in there." I squinted into the studio windows. They were tinted, but I was sure I saw little pinpricks of light inside.

"And you're sure this doesn't cost anything?" Lily said. She was hanging back uncertainly. "We're not going to show up and have to sit through somebody's PowerPoint and then get guilt tripped into blowing fifty bucks on essential oils, right?"

I tried the door to the studio, which swung open.

No one was at the receptionist desk. The little onsite daycare with its culturally questionable teepee playhouse was dark and silent, with that eerie cast play spaces have when no one's there to play. But I could hear quiet shuffling in the studio.

"This is nuts," Lily said under her breath, but we both kicked off our shoes and stashed them in the cubbies with our wallets and car keys.

"Hey," she said. "I brought you some of these." She handed me a pair of pink grippy socks. "They really do make it a lot easier."

"Thanks," I said, touched by the gesture.

"All right, let's go feed right into the unfair and unrealistic expectations American society places on new moms," she said.

I rolled my eyes at her, but the ease of the joking, the good-natured ribbing, felt like a bubble bath. It had been too long since I'd felt like someone's friend.

The barre studio's overhead lights were off, but there were soft recessed corner lights on. It gave the room an anticipatory, sacred feeling, like an empty church before midnight mass. Lily and I both looked around at the dozen or so other moms.

Lily, for once, had no snark.

If I felt out of place in the last barre class I went to, I was clearly in good company in this one. These women were train wrecks. Nobody looked like they'd showered anytime recently. Everyone's eyes seemed bloodshot, eyelids swollen, complexions sallow. Nobody had workout clothes or bras that fit right. More than one woman was openly weeping.

"Okay," Lily said quietly. "Okay, this is too much. These people need sleep, not core blasters."

"Let's just give it a try," I said. If this class was designed to help these women, surely it could help me, too.

Lily gasped in surprise at the sudden appearance of a woman behind her with little plastic bottles of water on a tray. She had that same odd gray stare of the person who'd invited us to this class.

"Take, drink," she said. *This is my blood, which is given for you,* my Episcopal childhood automatically finished for her.

"Uh, thanks," said Lily, and she took a huge swig out of one.

"You, too," the woman said.

I took a water bottle and noticed it had no label.

"Drink," the woman commanded, before moving to the next sad sack student.

I unscrewed the cap and raised it to my lips. Before I took a sip, though, my cell phone rattled against my thigh in my leggings' tight side pocket. Phones weren't allowed in the studio, so I shot a quick look around to be sure no one saw as I surreptitiously checked my lock screen.

<Where are you???> from Josh. <Please come home or at least let me know ur ok>

I thought about the message, and it occurred to me that Josh might think I was in trouble. Or having an affair. There was something deeply pleasurable in the idea of letting him worry for an hour. The thought that he might still have the capacity for jealousy felt tingly and delicious, almost like feeling desired.

Then, the music started.

It was a dark, low swell of a beat whose time signature I couldn't quite parse. There was something off about everything, its rhythm, its tonality. Some kind of experimental electronica, maybe.

Then, there was a soft plinking sound, almost like hail. I looked up from my phone.

Everyone else in the studio had dropped their empty water bottles to the ground.

I looked at Lily, but she was staring straight ahead, focused on some point that seemed to be beyond the mirrored front of the studio, where the mothers' faces were vacant in the low light.

I wanted Jenna and her ponytail and enthusiasm so much all of a sudden. There was no instructor at the front. But, even so, everyone started to move.

I looked around, a little panicked. The rest of the students were doing squats, so I tried to match their rhythm, but everyone was moving way too fast for a warmup, faster than I could keep up with, for sure.

The other women started rolling their shoulders back and forth in time with their squats, like they were starting to flap their wings.

I tried my best, but I couldn't keep up with the sweating, silent students pulsing in time with the unearthly music. A vocal track had started wailing and humming in discordant shrieks and woops that seemed to settle right behind my eyes, painfully lighting up all the dark and empty places in my skull.

I covered my ears instinctively. Now everyone had added some kind of belly roll to the sequence. It was the kind of thing kids would show off in middle school, a trick most people couldn't do, let alone a whole bunch of postpartum moms. Everyone was speeding up, to an impossible pace.

Then, I looked at Lily and an icy wash ran down my spine.

She was still staring straight ahead, moving through the routine in perfect time. But her eyes were rolled back in her head so that only the whites showed, like spider egg sacs.

"Lily," I said, and grabbed her hand.

My new friend shoved me away from her and continued the sequence. I fell down hard on my tail and felt my phone crunch. I was too stunned to be upset.

Another woman toppled backwards with a solid *thunk* as the back of her head slammed into the polished wood floor. Still, she kept thumping along in time with the music. She looked like someone was using a defibrillator on her, the way she spasmed upward into the air, her hips, shoulders, and abdomen still pulsing impossibly. A thin trickle of blood dribbled from the corner of her mouth.

"Fuck!" I shrieked. I grabbed Lily around the waist and tried to haul her out the door, but she was too strong and shook me off again. I stared at the class, where three or four more students had fallen.

If I couldn't get Lily out, I could at least get help.

I ran for the doors, shoving the push bar hard with both hands.

They were locked.

And for what felt like the first time since Micah's birth, my head was perfectly clear, my senses adrenaline-sharp. Every cell of my body was ready, waiting for instruction.

My only thought, crystalline-precise, was *survive.*

The first woman who'd fallen was still sprawled on her back and flopping up and down. She cleared the floor with each physically impossible pulse. Her neck looked broken and her head lolled listlessly. Her belly had swelled, like she was pregnant again, and there was a soft, dark purple wetness in the middle, like a bad spot on a piece of fruit or a patch of melting ice. It grew bigger with every horrifying flop.

And then she just split, like an orange being sectioned, or that time lapse of a decomposing fox.

It wasn't explosive, but somehow soft, in spite of the suddenness. She went still, her limbs and face a frame around the pool of red, pink, purple, and gray shining under the soft lights.

I'm sure I screamed, but no one else reacted.

More and more of the class collapsed. Lily was one of them. I stared helplessly at her convulsing on the ground, and then looked back at the first to fall.

There was a slender silver spire rising out of the crater where a real woman used to live. It slowly unfurled like a fern, twitching and shiny. Then, it started growing branches, two armlike appendages reaching for the ceiling, and then floating to its sides. The thing twisted.

There was a round head forming at its top, and fetal features emerged on the smooth silver surface.

Other silver spires began rising all around the room. There was a tremendous sweet and sour stink of blood and bowel contents. And my own vomit.

The spires were beautiful, terrifyingly beautiful. Now some of them were gingerly stepping out of their human yolk sacs, new silver legs spindly and uncertain, like baby deer. They were stepping toward me.

Survive.

I sprinted for the wall where the props were stored, like I'd once raced for the finish line of that half marathon while Josh cheered me on. I grabbed the biggest weight, this time—a blue ten pounder—and threw it with all my might at the studio's big glass window.

A spiderweb crack appeared, and I hurled myself at it.

The glass shattered with a musical tinkle. I tumbled down the ravine in a blur of pain and uncontrolled motion. But even while I crashed helplessly down toward who knew what physical calamity, all I could think about was the sheer relief of getting away from that music.

Eventually, there was stillness. Then, darkness.

And then nothing, until I found myself stuffed to the gills with lithium and listening numbly to the gentle psychiatrist working through my postpartum psychosis diagnosis with me.

I was hospitalized for six weeks. And the thing is, it helped. It truly did. I hadn't realized how bad things had gotten or how severe my depression had become. Of course it made sense that the entire barre class massacre had been a hallucination—how else could that make sense? There was no evidence that about twenty-five new mothers had met terrible, bloody ends birthing unspeakable silver horrors at a late-night exercise class.

I tried not to consider the implications of the pair of pink grippy socks in the plastic bag the hospital handed me at discharge.

I settled back in at home. Josh and I saw a couples counselor and worked out a reasonable division of household labor. Micah got bigger, and I got to know him as a person—a funny, gentle little person who loved cats and construction sites.

I might have gone my whole life believing the entire barre episode had been a product of a broken brain screaming for help if I hadn't come across Lily in my Instagram feed one day a couple of years later.

I stared at the photo in shock. I was positive it was Lily. But not the Lily I'd known. It was a photo of her in a deep yogic squat, her abs exposed and sharply defined, a bar across her back with an impressive amount of weight on it. Her child, looking like she was in the tail end of her toddler stage, played with magnetic tiles at her feet. The words "NO EXCUSES" appeared in white Helvetica at the top of the image.

It was definitely Lily's face.

But those silver eyes belonged to something else.

D.E.B.

H. V. Patterson

I hovered in the doorway as the nurse gestured into the room. It looked like every other examination room in the clinic: too white, an examination table and two stiff-backed chairs, a generic picture of the sun hovering over the sea. But something was wrong. I could feel it in the air, in the oppressive hum of the fluorescents.

"The doctor will be in shortly to discuss your test results," the nurse said.

Reluctantly, I stepped over the threshold. The nurse rolled back down the hallway, clicking softly. Nurses used the physical form deemed most efficient for their work, but the multitude of arms, the wheeling feet, and the flat screen where a face should be always unnerved me.

The door slid shut behind me. I tugged at it a few times. Locked. I didn't remember being locked in during my last mandated health check, but maybe they'd updated the protocols. They were always updating them, using complex algorithms I couldn't grasp, not with the limited biological hardware of my current brain.

I forced myself to take a deep breath, step away from the door, and sit in one of the hard-backed chairs. Strange, how there were always two of them. No one ever accompanied me to these appointments. Everyone went into their checkups alone. Maybe it was a calculated psychological attack, designed to intimidate patients. If it was, it always worked on me. I pressed my hands into my lap, willing them to stop trembling.

I focused on the picture, the sole source of color in the white and chrome room. Clouds partly obscured an orange-yellow sun as it hung on the horizon of an endless sea. Rising or setting, it was impossible to tell. The waves were stained red, brown, and purple, like bruised, rippling skin. I'd never seen the sea, but it looked indifferent and cruel in this picture.

The wall opposite me was filled by a SmartScreen. They were standard in every room, but I still turned my head to the side, as if avoiding direct eye contact would keep it from seeing me. Perhaps it was some outdated instinct to avoid catching a predator's gaze.

The SmartScreen flickered and hummed to life. A pleasant, pentatonic scale calculated to put me at ease filled the room. I stared longingly at the door, willing it to open.

"Well, hello there!" sang Debbie as the SmartScreen projected her into the room.

I couldn't help flinching. For the enhanced safety of all citizens, there was no such thing as privacy. For as long as I could remember, I'd been taught that only bad or dangerous people like our distant, uncivilized ancestors, ever wanted privacy. Debbie knew everyone's secrets and had access to all my personal data. I leaned as far back in my chair as I could, away from the flickering hologram.

"Hello, Debbie," I said through gritted teeth.

You couldn't ignore Debbie. I'd tried once, and she'd gotten bigger and bigger and louder and louder until her beaming face was my whole world and the air tasted of pixels.

"I'm glad you're with us today," Debbie said, voice soft and lilting. I'd grown up hearing that voice everywhere, but I'd only started to hate it after my graduation ceremony almost a year ago.

"I'm glad to be here, Debbie," I said dutifully, forcing myself to look the hologram in the eye.

Debbie was a marketing conglomerate's ideal of bland pleasantness. Modeled after composites of stock photos, she was designed to appeal to our creaturely selves with her wavy brown hair, warm eyes, and pleasantly symmetrical features. She appeared harmless, but the most sophisticated algorithms in the world couldn't hide her true purpose. She was here today to talk me into the Disembodiment Procedure.

I don't remember ever not knowing about the Disembodiment Procedure, or D.E.B for short. Like everyone else, I grew up in a CareHome with several dozen peers. From birth, Debbie's beaming presence floated before us, promising the wonders of D.E.B. before our infant brains had any concept of object permanence, much less embodiment and disembodiment. From the second we began breathing, Debbie was there, flitting amongst our caregivers, telling us stories about how wonderful it would be when we grew up, completed our D.E.B., and became responsible, adult members of the Pangaean Interglobal Alliance.

I looked down at my hands. The closer I got to losing them, the more miraculous they seemed. I knew my own physiology well and intimately understood my faults, redundancies, and inefficiencies as a carbon-based organism. We were encouraged from a young age to dislike our bodies, to alienate ourselves from them in preparation for adulthood. And yet, despite its fragility, despite my biochemical tendency towards anxiety, my acne and crooked teeth, my uneven hips and asymmetrical face, this body was mine. I couldn't hate it. My nails dug painfully into my palms, and I relished the sensation.

"You're twenty-six now," Debbie continued. "You've been eligible for your D.E.B Procedure for eleven months and three days. Is that correct?"

"You know it is," I said. I hated how Debbie was programmed to pretend she didn't know absolutely everything about us, to act like our friend.

"You know the D.E.B. Procedure is mandatory by twenty-eight?"

I nodded, throat tight. The closer I got to twenty-eight, the more I felt myself settling into this body, resisting the inevitable. I cried sometimes at night, listening to the relentless pounding of my heart, wishing I could inhabit my body for just a little longer.

Debbie tilted her head to the side, the motion too sudden and severe to be human.

"I'm sensing you have some reluctance regarding the procedure," she said.

I said nothing.

"You wrote an interesting essay a few years ago, arguing that the age for mandatory disembodiment should be raised to thirty-five."

I bit my lip. What had motivated me to write that stupid essay? The words had poured out of me like someone else was in control, like I was "possessed" by one of those demons humans used to believe lurked unseen amongst them, searching for souls to corrupt.

"It's an interesting argument," Debbie continued. "Sophisticated reasoning. But, you rely too heavily on pathos. You've seen the data. You know that by thirty-five most human brains have already lost much of their elasticity and started their slow decline into senescence. The changes are minor, not usually noticeable for decades, but they significantly impact success rates for D.E.B."

"I know." I unclenched my hands, took another deep breath, and forced myself to meet Debbie's eyes. "I know the success rate is 99.85% for individuals who undergo the procedure between twenty-five and twenty-eight. I know it's contraindicated to have the procedure outside of this age range."

"You're afraid," Debbie said, her soft voice a perfect facsimile of empathy. "It's natural for your body to fear its end, to want to prolong its biological integrity. But you're more than your body. The D.E.B. Procedure will elevate and enlighten you beyond the current constraints of your thinking. You can't even imagine, trapped in that fragile, decaying shell, what you're capable of becoming."

I'd heard this all before, over and over. I'd seen the numbers. But all future citizens of the Pangaean Interglobal Alliance had unfettered access to the surviving records of our past. I'd spent hours browsing the archives. I'd examined old advertisements, listened to presidents and dictators give speeches. I'd read books that made me cry even though I lacked context for half of what they discussed. Debbie was propaganda, and I knew that, like an animal bred for slaughter on a factory farm, I'd been raised to be complacent. The system was designed to make us long to shed our bodies and take our places in this false utopia.

I stared right into the soulless depths of Debbie's holographic eyes and saw no flicker of humanity in them.

There must be someone in there, some HR specialist running the program, tweaking code to my individual peculiarities and responses. The nurse who'd shown me into the examination room, the officials and teachers and caregivers who'd raised me—they were all once embodied like I was now. And yet, there was something so empty about them.

"I still have two years," I reminded Debbie. "Legally, I'm not required to report for disembodiment for two more years."

Two years: I would use them. I would lie in the sun like a feral cat. I'd roll in the grass until a dusting of green stained my skin and ants made a home in my hair. I'd swim in the nearby river, never mind the radioactive water. I'd fight crows for the cherries that grew outside my CareHome, relishing the sour bite of them on my tongue. This was my body and my life for two more precious years.

I sat as tall as I could, chin lifted, gaze level. Debbie grew bigger, maintaining eye contact. I didn't blink, and she didn't need to.

"Why even give us access to the archives if you don't want us to question how things are?" I asked.

"We want you to understand how terrible life used to be, how brutal it is to have a body, to be bound by the whims of physicality," Debbie answered. Maybe she read the sincerity in my microexpressions because she sounded almost kind. "We also want you to learn and question so your minds are in good shape, and you can become your best possible selves after the procedure."

I couldn't look at her anymore, so I closed my eyes. My lungs moved in and out, crude bellows delivering life-giving oxygen to my system. My stomach ached again, and I could feel a twinge in my hip. These chairs were always so uncomfortable.

"We aren't your enemy," Debbie continued. "We're all working together to create a kinder, more equal world."

I'd learned about war, racism, religious extremism, and nuclear genocide. In class, we'd seen starvation victims with bloated stomachs and hollowed eyes, dead and naked bodies mashed into bruised meat, cities vaporized in flashes of deadly light. Most of us wept when we started learning our history, a room of six-year-olds confronted by the ghosts of our collective past. We'd been taught the only way to exorcise what was rotten in humanity was to abandon our faulty bodies: violence was encoded into our very DNA, so goodbye DNA.

"Surely, there are things about your body you don't like?" Debbie pressed. "The acne and the scars it left, the way your hips aren't quite even—that must pain you. It'll only get worse the older you become. Embodied existence is just a losing battle against entropy."

They'd shown us that, too: what could go wrong with a body. As children, we'd wept at all the pain the world used to suffer, but as teenagers, we'd shrunk in revulsion from images of old age, the tracks it wore into the face, the way it bleached the hair and eyes of color and bent the spine. We'd seen graphic videos of knee replacements, cancer removals, stroke victims unable to care for themselves, locked inside their own heads. All around me, my peers had sneered, their faces twisted, contemptuous.

But in the archives, I'd seen pictures filled with people who were old, disabled, hurt by life, and they'd been smiling. Even when they didn't smile, even when they looked ready to collapse beneath the weight of existence, I'd seen something alive in their eyes, something intelligent and individual and fierce. When I stared into the mirror, I did see the blemishes on my face, my asymmetrical features, my sweat-shined skin. But I also saw a person looking back. I felt more kinship with the long-dead humans in those pictures and videos than with my caretakers and teachers and Debbie whirring beside me. And, maybe, given the choice, a lot of those long-dead people would've chosen D.E.B. Maybe they would've wanted a way out of their bodies. Or maybe they wouldn't. I didn't hate the existence of the D.E.B. Procedure in and of itself. What I resented was that I'd never had a choice: disembodiment was mandatory.

I opened my eyes and met Debbie's gaze once more.

"I want my two years," I said.

"You'll be alone," Debbie said. "Your CareHouse is empty; your peers are all gone."

"No more alone than before," I said.

Debbie smiled. This time, it wasn't a nice smile. Behind her pitiless eyes, I could sense programs rummaging through my data, calculating the best way to hurt me.

"Yes, you never did fit in, did you?"

A holographic projection of my graduation day flickered to life.

"Please, don't show it," I said.

"Why not?" Debbie asked. "It was your graduation day, and you were the top of your class. Surely, it's a good memory?"

"You know it isn't."

Debbie just smiled. I wanted to punch her, but there was nothing to punch. My traitorous eyes slid to the projection as the footage began to play.

The rendering of the worst day of my life was immaculate, more real than real. As I stood on the stage in the auditorium and delivered my valedictory speech, you could see every pore on my face, every displaced hair on my head, hear the defiance bleeding into each syllable as I spoke. I tried to tune out my earnest words, the snickers that gradually became jeers, but Debbie was merciless. The audio from my past rang out, clear and unavoidable as fate.

"—can't you see that life doesn't have to be like this, that D.E.B isn't the only way forward? Can't you see that we have years before we're required to turn ourselves over, years we can spend as we want? I know that most of you are going in for your procedures this month, and some of you are going in tomorrow! Why are you in such a rush? Why not—"

I wanted to shout a warning to my naïve, former self, but there was nothing I could do.

I flinched when the first rock hit my past self in the forehead. A trickle of blood flowed down her face. The scar it'd left was still present, a reminder I'd bear for my remaining time in this body.

"Still want your ugly body?" one of my peers taunted. Others laughed and joined in. Shouts of "Flesh-lover!" "Bio-freak!" "Blood-bag!" ricocheted from the auditorium's walls as rocks hidden in pockets and under chairs whizzed through the air. I watched my past self shield her face and turn appealing eyes towards the assembled caretakers and SmartScreens. They did nothing but gaze back, showing a play-by-play of my magnified, bloody face as the rocks struck. I watched my younger self's eyes widen when she realized this had been crudely and blatantly planned. As she realized that the caretakers must've noticed my peers gathering rocks, heard them whispering and giggling, and chosen to do nothing.

As I watched, my younger self dropped her arms, her mouth a grim line. I really think I would've died there, stoned to death like a witch or a Christian martyr.

But the SmartScreens chimed, and there was Debbie, maybe the same Debbie in the room with me today, maybe a different one, gently scolding my peers, telling them to drop their rocks. They grumbled but obeyed. They filed out of the auditorium and headed for the graduation party and the last meal some of them would ever eat.

My past self stood frozen, blood dripping into her eyes, smelling the roasted meat from a feast she wouldn't partake in. A nurse rolled over, checked her vitals, and slapped bandages over the worse cuts.

"It's a terrible thing, what happened," said the present Debbie in the examination room with me, her voice aligning perfectly, beat for beat, with the past Debbie in the auditorium. I gasped, momentarily unsure of where and when I was. "But can you really blame them?" The two Debbies continued in perfect synchronicity. "You know, deep down, that this cruelty is natural, human." Both Debbies smiled identical smiles. I blinked, and for a second, I was my past self again, feeling the drying blood trickling into my eyes and the hitch in my lungs as I struggled not to cry. "This is a final, hands-on lesson, just for you. Because none of the others seem to have sunk in."

Both Debbies' smiles widened. So many gleaming teeth in their blandly perfect faces. They were getting louder, their voices ringing through my skull, impossible to ignore. "This is why we have D.E.B. Our biology, our physical bodies, make us cruel, violent, and lazy. It isn't our fault that we're born so imperfect, but it is our fault if we refuse to evolve, if we promote a return to the archaic ways, to lives that were nasty, brutish, and short. Unproductive and greedy."

The examination room filled with flickering images and sounds, videos of people screaming and dying. I saw a child's brains drying on a wall; a man's fingers broken, one by one; a figure who looked just like me, hands tied, helpless to defend herself from a boisterous crowd.

It was too much, the images, the noise, the sound of the Debbies telling me that I was worthless, a parasite, a lazy piece of sentient meat mindlessly counting down the days in my pitiful, insignificant life. I slid onto the floor, pressing my hands over my ears, but it wasn't enough to drown them out.

"Salvation is before you, and you're a fool not to take it, not to beg to be freed from this mortal shell so that something decent and useful can be—"

"Shut up!" I screamed.

To my surprise, the noise stopped. Silence rang off the white walls. I raised my head. Only one Debbie remained, her hands neatly folded in front of her.

"Why are you doing this?" I asked, my voice soft and trembling. "Why are you pushing me to get the D.E.B now? After graduation, you left me alone. I still have two more years. What changed?"

"You always were so clever," Debbie said, crouching beside me. "It's because of your latest blood work."

"What about it?"

"Have you been feeling tired lately? A little . . . off?" she tilted her head slyly to the side.

"No," I lied.

I had felt more tired and nauseated than usual. But I'd figured it was a normal part of aging. I was the oldest embodied person I knew, the oldest I'd ever met. I didn't have anything to compare my experience to except for what the people of the past had left behind, and so much of that was a litany of suffering, pain, and hardship.

"You've developed a rare type of cancer," said Debbie, still smiling. "If untreated, death will result within six months."

The cold, white tile pressed against my bare legs as I gazed into Debbie's face, searching for some sign she was lying, but I knew she wasn't. Even now, I could feel the sickness creeping through me.

"But cancer is treatable," I said. "Aura had leukemia when she was seven. It was treated. She got better."

"Yes, it's treatable," Debbie conceded. "But, we will not be offering you treatment at this time."

"What?"

"Aura was a child, and childhood cancers are treated, as are all childhood illnesses, because children are important future assets," Debbie said. "A society without children will cease to exist. Adults, on the other hand, adults who are eligible for the D.E.B procedure—it isn't cost-effective to treat their bodily aliments."

"I don't understand," I said.

"The cancer hasn't compromised your brain. The probability for successful neural-synaptic mapping and upload is still 99.85%—if you're compliant."

"Compliant?" I stared at Debbie. This was new, something I hadn't heard before.

"It's why we do the . . . propaganda, as you call it," Debbie said. "Success is unpredictable in resistant subjects. We don't know why."

"So that's why you're here." I surged to my feet, glaring at Debbie.

"Please, try to calm yourself. We can keep talking—"

"I'm done listening to you. Let me out!"

I ran to the door. Still locked. I glanced wildly around the room.

"Your heart rate is elevated. Please attempt to calm yourself."

"Fuck you, Debbie!" I banged on the door's unyielding fiberglass.

Debbie sighed.

"Compliant or not, you'll be having your D.E.B Procedure momentarily," she said.

There was a gentle hiss behind me. I whirled around and saw white gas pouring from the vents in the ceiling.

"I'd rather die than have the procedure!" I screamed. "I'd rather let the cancer kill me slowly! Let me out!"

When the gas reached me, I tried to hold my breath, but I couldn't suppress my fragile, grotesque, beautiful body's need for oxygen. I staggered and slowly slumped to the floor.

Debbie hovered above me, her pixelated face coming in and out of focus.

"I know you find this distressing. But if the procedure is successful, you'll enjoy your new existence. Please, calm yourself."

I closed my eyes and focused on the tile, the soothing cold of it against my flushed cheek. It would be the last thing I ever felt.

I could do what Debbie said. I could relax, relinquish control, and focus on the positive aspects of D.E.B.: an existence so long, I'd be functionally immortal; freedom from pain; guaranteed work and utility. It would be so easy to admit I couldn't fight, couldn't change the way my world was, and let it happen.

I forced my eyes open. No, I wouldn't let them do this. I didn't believe there was anything waiting for me after death, and I didn't care. I'd had a good life. I'd listened to raucous crows, tasted fruit so sweet it sent a sting of pleasure right down to my fingertips, watched the sun rise and set in brilliant watercolor. The rain had poured over me as I dug my toes into the soil and stared at the gray sky, eyes dazzled by lightning, my whole body vibrating with thunder.

I will not wake up, I thought. *I will close my eyes, and this will be the end. I will not become like Debbie, like all the others. I have lived my life in this body, and I will die in it.*

I repeated this to myself over and over, with every ounce of strength and rage within me. A mantra, an incantation: *I can't have freedom, so I will have death.*

"Patient is ready for D.E.B. Procedure."

Darkness rolled across my vision. The last thing I saw before I lost consciousness: the sun forever sinking into the bruised sea.

CHILD BRIDE
Marsheila Rockwell

She was a child of twelve
By their reckoning
When she wed
Their much-loved king
A clause in a treaty
She had no hand in writing
And just eighteen
When he drank death
From a silvered cup
And left her his only heir

Her life the price of peace
They could not kill her
Instead they held her prisoner
On their gilded throne
Queen of nothing
Save the cold dark halls
And stairways
Connecting parapet to catacomb

So she bides her time
Waiting as her captors die off
One by one
And on the eve of every funeral
She descends to the tombs
Of their forgotton kings
Spits upon her husband's grave
And lays another thousand eggs

The Luthier's Muse
Julie Sevens

The *A* was off, a tiny discordancy stabbing her eardrums. Eugenia tightened the peg until it was perfect again. The long, clear notes poured sorrow from her soul, honeyed music dripping from the violin into the empty night. The vibrations against her throat carried her away from the damp, brick-lined basement.

Leather scuffed down the worn stone stairs to the workshop. The sound stopped her cold, her fingers suffocating the strings. Scurrying to the table, Eugenia lay the violin down on a stained wool blanket, a mother putting her baby to bed. The candle singed her fingers as she snuffed it, and the shadows lengthened on the violins hanging from hooks like fresh meat at the butcher. The door swung open as she perched on a rickety chair next to the hearth at the back of their arch-ceilinged burrow.

"Eugenia! My sweet little bird, still in the nest." Saverio was empty-handed, and Eugenia's stomach rumbled as her eyes skimmed the pot next to the fire. The thin, simmering broth alone wouldn't fix the hunger gnawing her bones.

Setting her mouth in a replica of blossoming contentment, she met his eyes. They were almost apologetic.

"Tomorrow, I'll deliver this violin back to Aldo. Then, I can get us a feast fit for a duchess." He patted the violin she'd been playing. The repair to the crack on its front had dried and set days ago.

Eugenia opened empty cupboards in the corner to see if a speck of dust would miraculously transform into another carrot or onion on the bare shelf.

The violin screeched under Saverio's wobbling fingers. She winced, her face turned toward the fire, and wondered if the tailor upstairs had gone home for the evening.

"These pegs won't tune!" He slapped the table. "They only want to pay for the new chinrest. Then when I bring it back, you know what Aldo'll say." He waggled his finger at her.

"You'll figure it out, Saverio," she said. "You always do."

Beaming, he nodded, his confidence restored. "This is why you're my muse." He held her face between his knotted hands, kissing her deeply, his tongue a worm in her mouth.

❖ ❖ ❖

Early the next morning, Eugenia woke and started the fire, shivering in front of it. Her bare feet were chilled against the rough stones of the floor. She brushed her hair until it gleamed, humming the tune her mother used to sing to her in the mornings.

Saverio snored in the bed while she fluttered around, tidying up the workshop. A tiny bit of graphite rubbed in the pegbox of the violin for Aldo got the pegs moving smoothly again, and it was ready to be delivered.

At midmorning, she paused and stood over him with her arms crossed. He was a brilliant luthier, but this skill sucked the life from all others, leaving the less glamorous aspects of his business fallow.

She kicked the bedpost, jiggling him from his slumber, and then went back to the table to count out supplies before he opened his eyes. He rolled over, moaning as he put one foot on the floor. Eugenia packed up the repaired violin as he rumbled around the back of the shop, getting dressed.

"What would I do without you?" The warm glimmer in his eye thawed her heart. It was true, of course, but she could say the same thing to him.

Four years ago, he'd found her soaking wet, cowering in his stairwell to hide from a pack of drunks who had chased her through the rainy dawn. Often, she'd remind herself of the pit of vipers outside when his affections became a suffocating fog. Her situation could be worse—had been worse.

He took the violin from her and headed out, pausing in the doorway. "I'll come back with a feast, promise."

She was alone again with the violins, admiring their coppery chestnut sheen in the lamplight. She reached up to pull her favorite down, a deep red instrument with a patterned rim of mother-of-pearl and ebony that assured it would sell soon.

A whistle on the stairs announced a customer. A woman carrying too many things struggled through the door and panted over to the table.

"Hello, dear. I'm supposed to pick up the master del Vecchio's violin. Been with you for repairs." Her sweet voice might talk a cow through the pain of calving.

"Of course," Eugenia said. She searched the tall shelves for the case tagged *L. del Vecchio* and plucked it from its cubby.

The servant opened it, peeking inside. "He needs some rosin for his bow, too."

Eugenia felt the woman's broad face studying her as she pulled two cakes of rosin from a drawer and wrapped them in paper.

"Thank you." The woman dug through another of her parcels. "Here, nobody will miss these from the shopping." She pressed two strips of candied orange peel into Eugenia's hands.

"I can't take these!" Eugenia stared at the sweets in her hand, her mouth watering. "Sure you won't get in trouble?"

"Must have been mis-weighed," she said, shrugging.

Eugenia held the door open for her.

"Take care," the woman said as she passed. The syllables had too much heft to them for an ordinary parting pleasantry. The woman's eyes lingered on her for an extra beat.

As soon as the door closed, Eugenia marveled at the candied orange peels.

She took a tiny nibble, holding it in her mouth, savoring every crystal of gleaming sugar. The scent of the citrus tantalized her, and though she meant to save one for later, she ate them both. The lingering flavor whispered a song to her and she picked up the violin to play.

Above her, through the slatted green shutters recessed from the street, she heard a loud voice discussing the song. She played softer, eavesdropping, hungry for an audience. Other than Saverio—when he would still give her lessons to tell her everything she was doing wrong—she hadn't heard anyone's reaction to her playing.

"Just listen to Saverio play. Such a sweet melody," the loud woman said.

"Why won't he come play at the palace? Surely the duke's invited him," her companion said.

Eugenia imagined the woman leaning in conspiratorially as they gossiped.

"He hasn't let *anyone* see him play in years."

❖ ❖ ❖

True to his word, Saverio returned late in the afternoon laden with a feast. A boy carrying two hunks of wood trailed him. The boy set down his delivery and bounced away without a word, his knobby knees catapulting him back up the street.

The food rolled across the table as Saverio set it down. Eugenia dug through it: fresh crusty bread, a wheel of cheese, figs, roast pigeon. Her stomach growled, but he turned back to the wood, the blank slate of a new violin.

"Come here, come here!" He handed her a mug of wine and wrapped his arm around her waist.

"This violin will be perfect. My best one yet, every angle and curve inspired by you." His breath was hot on her chest as he laid his head against her. "I've got the perfect wood from Paneveggio, just excellent. Look!" He pointed at the spruce slab he hadn't yet begun to carve. His hands slid across her body, her neck, her waist, the curves of her shoulders.

"And the fancy maple?" she said, her hand on the second slice of wood.

Holding the plank up to his ear, he rapped his knuckles on it. "It's going to sound flawless when I'm done. I'll have the carcass to make the strings and everything tomorrow." The process of making strings from a freshly slaughtered sheep was never her favorite. Eugenia wrinkled her nose at the thought of the intestines spilling out, still warm.

He pulled apart the waves of linen fabric tucked into the laced front of her bodice, burying his face, running his nose along the hidden skin of her breast. Admiring a lock of her hair between his fingers, Saverio sighed. The strands slipped from his hand.

"I need to make the bow." His eyes were still on her hair. "And, I was wondering," he continued with a wince.

Eugenia gathered her hair in her hand and squeezed the thickness of it.

"How much of it?" she said.

His face shone as he examined her hair again. He lifted some of the golden strands, letting them cascade in a waterfall. He held up the long bow stick, measuring it against her hair.

"I only need this much." A thick lock was pinched in his hand, the diameter of a finger. "You'll barely notice."

Eugenia assented with a quiet nod.

Swooping at her with a blade, he sliced off the lock from the edge of her forehead before she could suggest a less obvious section. He took his prize back to the bow stick as her hand flew up to investigate the damage. The stubbly ends of the newly shorn patch poked at her fingers above her forehead, like daffodils rising from the frozen ground in the spring.

"Perfect!" he said. He turned back to her to display the hair against the bow stick, the extra length flowing from the sides.

He saw her face, her hand in her hair. "It doesn't even look like anything's missing."

She held back tears as he came back to her and took her hands in his.

"Please forgive me." He pressed his forehead to hers. The cut hair poked into his bald forehead. "It's worth it. And you're beautiful. Beautiful, beautiful."

He cajoled her to the table, where the feast waited for them, and Eugenia decided her irritation about the haircut would keep better than the food would. The gathering storm behind her green eyes dissipated.

Cutting into the wheel of cheese released a deep, earthy smell that pushed aside the cold breeze on her scalp. They ate like two street urchins catching the baker's scraps in the evenings. The wine in the pitcher disappeared into their bellies, giggles interrupting the feast.

Saverio slopped more wine into her cup. The bitter sediment in the bottom clung to her mouth, rough on her palate. She pressed the heel of her palm to her temple, her head woozy from the wine. Grazing the stubble sent a flash of bile rising from her stomach, but she swallowed it back down.

He led her to the bed, nestled the blankets up around her. He kissed her forehead, lingering on her brow.

"You rest, little sparrow." As her eyes closed, she watched him begin carving the spruce for the front of his already-treasured violin. A mountain of thin-curled wood shavings formed around him as he worked.

❖ ❖ ❖

"We have to work quickly, Eugenia, my muse. Can't let it cool or the strings will have little holes from the veins." His blade sliced cleanly through the pale belly of the still-warm carcass, hidden in the darkest back corner of the workshop reserved for the more unpleasant parts of violin making. Tendrils of steam curled from the wound, like breath on a cold morning.

Eugenia's stomach turned as the entrails spilled into a bowl of cold water. Saverio's hands ran the length of the intestines to clean them, the offal splashing into the water. The blade slid along, scraping the fat away until they were cleaned.

Satisfied, he let the guts drip water back into the bowl, and then coiled them in a pail of salt. Eugenia stared at him. The eye-watering stench filled the shop, but he wouldn't open the shutters, keeping the door barred.

He tied the carcass up from the beam, slitting its throat and letting the blood drain into an old cooking pot.

"Next, we'll skin it. Can't waste a good source of hide glue." He smacked his chapped lips together. She remembered her father skinning coneys, stripping their fur like a sweater to leave a naked rabbit, shining and ready for roasting. The sharp blade Saverio had used on Eugenia's hair slid under the skin, separating it, peeling it away in chunks, nothing like the clean pull of a hunt. The layers of tissue and red muscle below were revealed, the flower's blossom showing as the bud fell away.

Saverio lay the skin in chunks across the dining table, scraping it clean with a spoon. Eugenia hovered over the pile of skin, her face ashen. It was nearly translucent, the inside-out skin surreal and rubbery. He chopped it into even smaller pieces, ready to dry and then boil into a gray, gelatinous soup.

Warmed over a candle, later, he'd dip a brush in it to apply the hot hide glue at the seams and joints of a new instrument.

Eugenia grimaced as he swept some of the trimmings away with the back of his hand and set last night's bread on the table where the skins had been. He fetched a plate and tore off a hunk, dipping it in the sour dregs of wine from last night. Across from him, she watched the crumbs of the bread fall on his shirt.

The plate of crumbs sat on the table as Saverio went back to work.

"We're almost done, sweet little bird. Almost," he said, holding her cold fingers in his.

When he pulled the carcass down from the hooks in the ceiling, the head stayed stiffly afloat, not touching the table. The pail of drained blood tripped him, stubbing his toe as he stepped around it. A flash of anger crossed his face, chasing the pain, and he feinted at the bucket. He took a deep breath, staring at his reflection in the surface, and carried it across the workshop to the front door to dump it outside. As he paused to unbar and open the door, scarlet sloshed down the front of his leather apron.

The head had so far been spared from Saverio's flaying. Anemic and chalky, its skin didn't fit right over the bone beneath anymore. Eugenia studied the wide green eyes. They were starting to cloud; clear marbles hiding trails of fog until held up to the light.

Saverio returned, blood dripping from the bottom of his apron. "Now, where were we?"

He chopped off the hair and tied the blond strands in hanks to hang in the shop until needed to someday replace the bow strings. The luthier stroked the hair, its loose ends curling against the wall like vines.

Running his fingers along the stiff jawline, he found a soft spot at the base of the neck. He sank his blade in, slicing the head away, his blade working back and forth like a bow. When he was done salvaging what he needed for the violin, he put the bones he wanted to keep in hot water to strip them of their flesh.

Eugenia watched the simmering pot in the hearth, the hunks of flesh and bone that had been hers now reduced to materials for the luthier.

Her skull and hands bobbed in the thick stew as the muscle and meat on them loosened. Familiar fingers drifted in the water, the freckle on her knuckle distorting as her skin began to dislodge. A cloudy green eye floated to the top of the pot, rolling in the heavy seas, and she gazed at her own pupil.

Saverio dropped on his knees to the hard stone by the hearth, wailing an apology to her. Behind him, Eugenia sat in her chair by the fire, watching as he begged the pot for forgiveness, her blood still dripping from his leather apron.

❖ ❖ ❖

Days of feverish carving passed, Saverio barely eating, sleeping when his head lolled and nodded off over his work. The spruce from Paneveggio neared its final form as the front of the violin, missing only the scrolled cutouts. Fine stripes of caramel-colored wood joined along the center of the back piece. When he held it to his ear and tapped, the sound was flawless.

He winked at Eugenia's skull, the beige and yellow bones of her eye sockets watching him pull her intestines across the splitting horn, ripping them into two long strands. "The right sides, we'll use for the violin strings. The left, I'll sell for cello strings. Different thicknesses, you know."

The strings, her skull, her fingerbones; these final remains went into the oven behind the slaughtering table. In the bottom of the stove, he piled chalky yellow pebbles of brimstone. Brilliant blue and lilac flames leapt from the brimstone when he lit it. Eugenia choked on the smell, the deep acidic burning, as the smoke coated her bones. Tendrils of it inside her skull crawled through her nose and ears. Even when she fled from her remains, she could feel the hot smoke eating at her.

After long hours purifying in sulfuric fumes, Saverio retrieved her from the oven shelf. The ribbons of her intestines were clean, ready to be twisted and pulled into strings. Her skull and fingers had whitened in the heat of the brimstone.

Saverio caressed the top of her skull, cradling it.

"I'm sorry, my love. I wish there had been another way." He exhaled, his eyes brimming. "This will be the most perfect violin in the world. But it can only be that with your help. I didn't have a choice." He kissed the top of her skull, the warmth of his lips stinging her forehead.

Then, he put her skull on a shelf in the corner of the workshop, leaving her to watch.

❖ ❖ ❖

The sun cut through the slats in the shutters, the finished violin glossy and shining. Saverio had spent long hours carving her finger bones into tuning pegs, tiny little sparrows flying on each one. The hide glue made from the soupy broth of her skin held the wood together at the seams, and he had finally strung it.

The finished violin had spent weeks curing, Saverio afraid to touch it. Many times, he walked up to the violin, hovered a hand out, withdrew it. Lying awake at night, he would stare at it. The past few days he had been talking to it, arguing with it. Sometimes he'd look at her skull in the corner, and talk to her, too, though she hadn't figured out yet a way to respond.

Now, he picked up the bow, rubbed the strands of her hair with rosin again. He sniffed at the hair, smelling the scent of her lingering there. Drawing in a breath that puffed his chest, holding it as though he would dive underwater, he strode to the violin and picked it up.

The bow hummed, its golden strands singing. He tightened a fingerbone peg, loosened another, testing the tuning. Eugenia lost her patience, wishing she could make him stop fumbling.

The tuning fell into place in the exact way she hoped it would, the pegs moving at her fingertips. The bow drew across the strings again, a pure, beautiful note resounding from the luthier's workshop. The music emanated from deep within her; the vibrations resonated through her skin.

He threw open the shutters, the street above filled with boots and shoes passing by. The violin played again, a sweet melody flowing from it. His clumsy hands slid across her with that familiar sense of ownership they had always had. Some of the shoes paused, gathering around the window.

Whenever he missed the angle or the fingering, Eugenia corrected the sound. The strings vibrated at her command, Saverio's body a puppet holding the violin. She was the one giving the lessons now, correcting the form, demanding the proper fingering.

"I told you he was great," one of the spectators crouched on the street said.

The music surged, storm clouds gathering, the violin resisting the song he wanted to play. She reached out from the instrument, gripping his hands, his neck, pinning him in place. Saverio's arm jerked back and forth. Outside, the crowd thickened, clotting the street. She paused and let them applaud.

His chest heaved; his pulse pounded against the ribs of the violin. He was trying to push away, a coney in a snare, trapped. His muscles tightened away from her, as hers often had when she forced herself not to recoil from his touch. Eugenia clamped down tighter.

The violin erupted again, Eugenia's anger bursting into song. The terrified luthier clung to the bow as it whipped his arm. His shoulder popped from its socket, the arm now a loose rag hanging from the bow. The calluses on his fingers cracked and bled on the strings as she forced them into position on the neck.

His body would break long before the music stopped.

THE MAGICIAN ON HIS DEATHBED
J.M. Sedlock

The luster of magic comes from ignorance. When people come to my shows, some part of them knows they are being tricked, the wool over their eyes tied with nimble hands and vivacious cadence, but they grab at ignorance as if it is the lifeblood that sustains them. I seduce them into it. I am the pied piper, leading them not into death but childlike wonder. Even the ones who strain themselves to work out the methods of my deceptions want to believe the things I do are real.

And so it may come as a surprise to you that I was lied to as well. A performer of my caliber, an apprentice of stage magic and parlor tricks since I was a boy, fell into a trap that was my undoing. My own ignorance made me haughty, my own pride in my skills a fool, and my own impatience a lantern which guided me to my current predicament.

A young man approached me after a show. The crowd's enthusiasm had left me floating high above kings and gods, and I knew the theatre would book me again. The stranger came to me while I was enjoying my one nightly cigarette backstage. He was short, perhaps a bit underfed, and wore a grin I mistook for unrestrained excitement.

"Sir," he said in a voice that now sounds like hissing adders when I recall it. "You are quite the showman, and I enjoyed your tricks. May I show you some of my own?"

His eagerness gave me enough pause not to send him away with my typical bluntness. I smiled, put out my cigarette, and extended my hand to the lad. He looked at it but did not return the gesture, his face the very picture of a most peculiar puzzlement. Despite the lack of any recognizable accent, I assumed he must be foreign, and I let the social faux pas slide without comment.

"I'm sorry to disappoint you, but I already have an assistant, and I'm not looking to take on another."

I looked over my shoulder and gestured to my grown son, his hands so like my own tending to the care of our show rabbits.

"Ah, you are mistaken," said the boy. And when I turned, there was no boy, but an old man. He had the face of someone used to hardship, wrinkles and spots as innumerable as the stars, but his grin told of a life with nothing but play and glee. I jumped in my skin, my mouth agape, feeling quite like a fish with a hook through its bloody cheek. My expression made the old man's grin stretch beyond the limits of where his mouth should have been.

"You see," he began before I had quite gathered my wits from the floor, "I am not asking for your guidance, but rather offering my own."

At that I felt a keen prickling of rage. I assumed that they must be a father and son pair, some newcomers to the industry trying to make their mark by humiliating their betters. It was disappointing; had they made some genuine attempt at humility and camaraderie, I would have been more than happy to introduce them.

I steeled my face.

"Your boyish prank is not impressive. Tell your accomplice that I am not interested in such juvenile affairs."

I surveyed the few people milling about for the mischievous boy's face; but, failing to spot him, I felt my anger boil down to mild annoyance. Whatever its nature, the trick had been uncovered, and the boy would be found eventually. I found great satisfaction in the thought of barring them both from the theatre.

The old man, his face still stretched in some mockery of delight, leaned forward and wiggled his thick white brows.

"Would you like to see it again?"

I sneered, and I saw the man's gaze drop down to my mouth, his eyes ticking along each shiny tooth as if appraising their value.

"You are a fool," I replied with as much venom as I could muster, "and do not think for a second that we are equals."

Before I could stop him or even cry out to call attention to his audacious behavior, the old man's arm shot out with terrifying speed and gripped my hand with his own. His skin was rough against mine, a sample of sandpaper against fine silk.

"It was a fine thing, you know. A clever thing. Putting some of your own staff in the crowd like that. But don't you think having your wife faint was a tad much, a bit gauche? I certainly thought so."

I laughed. The ruse, if it could even be called such a thing, was common practice in the industry, and so the strongest ignorance of it just illuminated his woeful lack of experience.

"And what of it? You know nothing of the craft, sir, so you have no right to insult my methods."

The man's eyebrows rose and crinkled together. If not for the grin still on his face, which somehow stayed stretched taut as he spoke, I would have thought he looked confused.

"Insult you? I have only called you fine and clever, but you called me a fool. It is you who insulted me, my friend."

Finding my mouth dry of any rebuttal, I yanked my hand free and walked away from the man without another word. I was done entertaining this childish volley of wit with someone who was clearly a delinquent unworthy of my time. However, it seemed that the pair was not quite done with me. Before I reached the door, I heard the old man's laugh right in my ear, and his voice whispered: "a fool, eh?"

I turned so quickly that the ache in my neck is still with me today, but he had not moved. He waved as I fled the room, feeling much less triumphant than before.

Later that night, my son reported that he had not seen the boy backstage, nor had he seen anyone matching his description in the theatre at all. When I asked about the old man, his whole face narrowed.

"I saw him," he said, "but I can't picture him now."

During the time when I should have been asleep, and I always slept peacefully, my mind was in a chokehold. The evening's events played over and over in my mind as my wife slept beside me.

I could not let go of that man. At first, I thought I was still angry, but then I realized it was something else entirely: envy as green as sickness.

How had he done it?

No matter how many times I turned over the trick, examining every angle and possibility, I could not figure it out. The ruse before my humiliating exit could be explained away by a skilled ventriloquist, but the boy . . .

Unless my staff were complicit, there was no way for them to switch without my notice. The room was too fast, the people too many, and my eyes too keen. And if not my staff, it seemed an odd prank for the theatre to pull on one of their most lucrative performers. With all my thought experiments turning up nothing, I fell into an uneasy sleep.

It was not until the morning that the trouble started, and I began to see the hell my life would become.

At the time, I attributed my first incident to tiredness, but hindsight revealed the spiral of falling blocks with my doom at its center. I fumbled with my razor; not an unusual incident by any means, but a sudden disconnect between my hand and my mind led the razor down my neck at such an alarming angle that a surging stream of blood ran down over the hill of my collarbone and dripped onto the floor.

Later, I would wonder about that blood, about how it seemed thicker and darker than usual. Was this, too, a lie? Or was I dying of some human condition the whole time?

In the moment, however, I patched myself up and finished my shave. My neck was marred for weeks, each stare a wound to the fortified castle of pride I had built up since boyhood.

The following weeks brought me no comfort. My slips and fumbles became regular and unnerving occurrences, resulting in a collection of wounds and bruises. A stranger on the street remarked that I looked like a battered woman, to which my family lowered their eyes in shame. Smiles became a rare currency in our household; it was much more common to see my wife and son exchange worried glances, or for someone to yelp at the sight of a new addition to my living canvas of scabs and jagged scars.

There was one instance where the wound of my clumsiness was not to my body, but to my pride. Before all this nonsense began, I had been hired to perform simple feats of magic at a child's ninth birthday party. The day edged closer, having slipped my mind in lieu of the obvious, until it was too late to cancel without damaging my reputation. While I was being paid, the party was for the daughter of a very wealthy gentleman, and I knew word of my failure would spread if I failed to appear at the event.

However, much to my scarlet-cheeked embarrassment, I did not make it past my first trick. It was a simple optical illusion in which I placed one of our trained rabbits into a wooden box; the rabbit, being clever and plied with vegetables, would nose its way under a false bottom in the box, therefore giving the illusion that it had disappeared. The trick had been in my repertoire for most of my career, and children generally found it delightful. However, when I went to open the box painted in colorful occult symbols, I found that I simply could not.

In a gesture of comedy, I took off my hat and placed the rabbit inside so I could fiddle with the box using both hands.

My hands would not obey me. When I tried to move my thumb up, it moved down, and when I tried to push the clasp down, my whole hand scrambled to the top of the box and forced the pads of my fingers along the wood until I gave myself a splinter! I stood, my mouth simultaneously scrunched and agape, as the children laughed and pointed.

As if I needed another feather in my cap, I knocked over the stool where my hat was sitting as I turned away from the crowd. The bunny toppled out of it and ran away into the bushes: our efforts to locate her were futile.

❖ ❖ ❖

After that dreadful affair, my wife put her foot down and refused to book more shows until I saw a doctor. I did as she bid with the shameful reluctance of any sophisticated man taking orders from his wife, but the doctor had nothing remarkable to say. He concluded I was of sound body, and that the tremors must simply be a newly awakened nervous disorder from my expanding career. He prescribed me a course of sedatives to take before my shows, remarking that all my fears would become "edged with clouds and more pleasant times."

Oh, if I could have been so lucky.

That Friday evening, I had a show in the same theatre where I saw the old man and his accomplice. Word of my disastrous fortune had not spread far enough to affect my bookings just yet.

It went well. The house was packed, intermission came and went, and the mysterious tremors had all but vanished. With the doctor's funny little pills in my arsenal, I was well armed with youth and charisma. Any hint of nerves I may have felt were politely crushed under the weight of a sweet, cotton cloud around my mind. By the time I was gearing up for my finale, I had come to understand how gods felt with followers prostrate at their feet.

I needed a volunteer for my final act, and the sea of hands that went up at my request brought such a smile to my face. My eyes searched until I found my wife, a beautiful woman decked out in the many-layered organza dress popular amongst theatre-going women of the day. She was bright, painfully so under the stage lights, and she climbed up on stage to stand beside me. The room was soft and full of light the color of taffy and party dresses, and my face bore a smile so wide that my cheeks ached for days afterwards.

In my hand, I knew I held a soft green ribbon around which I had earlier tied an invisible string. Backstage, my son held the other end of the string, and he would pull it once he received my signal disguised with occult hand gestures. It would appear to the crowd that the ribbon, which was first tied prettily around my wife's, had been undone by some phantom or force of telekinesis. And for an edge of the dramatic, small and harmless pyrotechnic effects along the ribbon would demonstrate the supernatural effort of such a feat.

I had the ribbon clutched in my hand, and I knew it was my hand. Only I commanded it to move and flex, to demonstrate to my audience that there was no trickery around the ribbon between my fingers. I walked to my wife and began to tie the ribbon with my hands, my flesh and blood hands with which I built my career, my life, and my marriage.

But they were not my hands, really, not at all. If I had any choice in the matter, I would not have tightened the ribbon to the point that she began choking, nor would I have given up on that effort entirely and lunged forward to throttle her.

And then my wife was not a woman at all, but a rabbit, and my hands squeezed with titan-like strength. Her woman-rabbit's bones cracked beneath them. Blood dribbled from her mouth onto my starched cuffs, and finally—finally!—I let her go.

The not-rabbit woman in her white organza monstrosity fell to the ground dead. My hands had made a corpse of her.

This I would be told later, for all I could focus on then was my hands. They were all bent and pressed in wrong angles from the labor of inhuman strength. Behind me, the crowd fled. They trampled over each other to get away from the sight newspapers would later call "most unholy."

I stared at my hands, taking in their limpness, their inability to do anything I commanded, and I began to laugh; amidst the screaming and animalistic shoving of bodies, I laughed until my throat strained like a rope pulled taut.

The ugly sound cut off in my chest as soon as I heard the applause.

I turned, fighting my heaving lungs and the deep pain in my hands that would become permanent, and he was there. My devil! My haunting. My personal affliction. His young, unmarred hands and his boy face mocked me from the theatre's very center seat.

"You," I rasped. "Please, my hands, I can't move them."

"I know," he said, standing. "I took them. Consider it an insult repaid."

He came to the edge of the stage, his hands turned upwards to catch the tears that flew from my eyes as I stumbled forward. They hit his skin, and I looked up to see a blurred vision of two different faces attempting to be one. The old man's wrinkles swam across his face like worms, unable to settle on the boy's young skin, and the teeth behind his wide grin gleamed with the manufactured whiteness of dentures.

I crawled forward until my head knocked against his shoulder, my heaving sobs soaking his shirt. My dignity, my pride, and my anger had fled; I saw no recourse except for throwing myself at the mercy of this creature.

"I don't know what you are, but I know that I've offended you, and I would flay myself alive in the boiling pits of damnation for the chance to take back my insults. Please—creature, devil, whatever you may be, forgive me!"

I felt his smile against my scalp, and his hands rose up to pet my back.

"You're forgiven, sweet thing. Stop those dreadful tears."

I dragged myself up, my face an ugly and pitiful sight, and tried to grip his shirt with my mangled fingers.

"Then fix me, please! Fix me! Haven't I suffered enough for you, foul thing?"

The creature held my eyes as his hand rose further, traveling up the back of my neck to grip my hair in his fist. His expression was gentle, perhaps even sympathetic, as his other hand patted my cheek.

"I forgive you, but I did not say I would help you."

He left me there, then, but I did not see him go.

My story kept me out of prison, but I could not avoid justice in its entirety. After hearing my account, the honorable judge sentenced me to this institute for hospice, madmen, and other eccentrics the country does not know what to do with.

I keep to myself. I have no other choice; the ones who are lucid enough to read the news don't want anything to do with me, and the ones caught in their own minds are afraid of me. They all know the old man with the boy's face underneath never quite left.

I take no visitors. My son has attempted to see me, but I turn him away every time. I must use all my time to gather my thoughts and put this account down on paper, for I do not have much time to spare. My only company is the rage I have managed to gather against my torturer. All my efforts, all the hours I spent on my knees praying to his image, he continues to punish me. I use his unyielding arrogance as a whetstone for my own, so that I may have some will to fight on.

There are times when I think I hear his voice or his laugh, usually when I wake up with my hands gripping my throat so tight that they leave bruises.

I do not know when my end will come, but I suspect it will be soon, and by my own hand in a way priests cannot damn me for. And if I see him again, I will take him with me, even if I must gnaw our path down to hell.

I Am a Weapon
Grace R. Reynolds

My body's worth
Is gilded in steel, scintillating under
Fluorescent lights that hurt my eyes,
And I wonder where dignity hides
For mothers like me, bound
In shackles behind the doors
Of 'Labor and Delivery.'

They say I am
A menace; that I am
A weapon; that I am
A vessel standing in a pool
Of amniotic fluid dripping past my knees—

Nevermind the restraints,
Or dangers that scream in defiance
Against best practices in medicine.
My care is paid for in blood,

Crimson insurance
Reaped by politicians
From taxpayers, their willingness
To ignore the risks that threaten
The pulp of flesh growing
Inside this body;

Their body;

My body,
But I am a weapon.

A correctional officer speaks for me.

BLEEDING AT HER ROOTS
Sarah Jane Huntington

'Wives, submit yourselves unto your own husbands, as unto the Lord,' —Ephesians 5:22.

NO. NO. NO.

❖ ❖ ❖

Anna assesses the horizon for a new escape route, a weak spot. The jagged hills are no use, she's tried twice and both times, even with darkness and stealth as a cover and guide, she was caught and dragged back, kicking and screaming.

The security cameras are the problem. Cold and paranoid electronic eyes watch every move.

She begins to wonder if the only way out might be death. The thing inside her belly writhes and rebels against her bitter thoughts.

The pain is crippling. Her spine, her legs, and her entire body hurt in waves that feel like wild mutilation. She places a hand on her swollen stomach, not to comfort the monster inside, the parasite, but to silence it. She presses down forcefully. She hates it, *hates* it. An invader, an enemy within.

"Sit up straight," her mother hisses down her ear. "Grace and poise at all times."

"No," she instinctively snaps.

This wicked situation, it's all her mother's fault, she's the one who insisted they sell up and move to barren lands to follow a fraudulent prophet. She swore it would be a peaceful community, away from crime and with tranquility as a permanent companion.

That was two years ago. She was thirteen when they arrived, a child led along without choices. Her sole parent was obsessed with the man people believe God himself has chosen as an earthly voice.

Anna believes she belongs to the other, if any. The one who rebelled and plummeted in the very beginning, the dark one, the trickster with the hooves and horns.

The compound must be owned by evil; it surely contains all manner of wrongdoing.

At first, the land and the people on it were friendly and welcoming. Yes, she had to wear long dresses and listen to fire and brimstone teachings, but there were other girls her own age, and friendships were made. Were.

She hasn't seen any of them for four months. Not since she was married off to the prophet himself and told the role was an honor. Her voice, her body, and her personality are being taken, stolen piece by piece.

Her life consists of sewing and cleaning, washing and cooking. Jobs only a female should do, according to made-up scriptures molded into a reverse shape.

Rules, order, structure, patriarchal systems, and the subjugation of women. Even now, the prophet, the disgusting man who is old enough to be her grandfather, preaches with a vile, twisted tongue of hatred.

"The sons of Adam are superior, the daughters of Eve exist for the purposes of temptation and breeding only."

His words are hypocritical nonsense. Anna knew enough of the world before they moved to recognize the scent of bullshit. Men like him, they fear women. They lack control of their own desires and secret, forbidden perversions. A woman kept in metaphorical chains is the only kind they will tolerate. Mouths closed and legs open.

Anger begins to rise. Her blood feels boiling hot and her skin erupts with the sensation of electricity.

It's hell inside the cult, because that's exactly what it is, a cult of the most wicked teachings with layers of darkness hidden.

She has to get out before the thing in her womb is born. If she leaves, she can beg doctors to remove it, medical experts will save her. Police officers will listen. Underage marriage and forced sexual unions. She will plead until she has salvation and beg until hope sparks and creates redemption.

"Women should be seen and not heard," the prophet continues. "They should only be submissive."

The words rattle around her mind. She opens her mouth to speak, to shout and scream. Her words fail and die like a damp match that won't spark.

"Don't you dare," her mother, sensing her rebellion, warns her.

Mother, by name only. Two syllables that used to invoke the feeling of love, of comfort, not betrayal. The woman damned her and did so willingly.

"Perfect wives," the prophet continues with a sneer worthy of a sick killer. "Should be controlled and silenced, kept to heel, like a dog. A man should enjoy his wives, not hear them complaining."

Small applause breaks out and echoes. The meeting room she sits in is one of many wooden buildings on the compound. The cult itself consists of almost one hundred people with elders made up solely of older men. Men with eyes that show lust for innocent children.

Anna jolts in her seat. There is a fire in her, a supervolcano, an inferno. It's all too much. Her stomach ripples and her flesh burns as if hot flames and lava already swarm. Bitterness, hatred, intolerance—multiple emotions bombard her until they simmer and boil over.

"NO," she cries. "No more. You're no one, none of you are. You're nothing. It's all lies!"

Her mother is the first to move. Others soon follow until a cascade of people falls back.

Now she sits alone, afraid. The spotlight, the eyes of the prophet of perversion land on her. Him, with his evil ways. She heard him chanting strange and dark languages along with the elders, down in the cellar the night she grew afraid and ran, the night she was caught and forced into marriage. They made her lie down in a circle of strange symbols, drugging her until consciousness was lost.

"The end times are upon us and yet, you, a woman, call me nothing? How dare you speak," he growls. Spit flies from his mouth and dribbles down his chin. He is utterly repulsive.

She's done it now, she knows what comes next.

Defiant, she tries to stand. Who can help her? Who can rescue her, take her away?

If God does exist, he has chosen to look away.

An enemy crawls in her womb, one the prophet put there, and soon, it will kill her. She will not be submissive, she would rather the grim reaper arrive and take her.

"Put her in the hole," the man yells. Power is his drug of choice, violation, his dessert.

Strong arms reach for her, yank and pull. Further suffering, more hell. She kicks and tries to bite, hisses and scratches.

Her body is her own, should be. Her mind belongs to her and will not be broken or manipulated, she is not a puppet, and she is not her mother.

"I hate you all," she screams as she is dragged away. Rage. Female rage. There is no greater power known.

❖ ❖ ❖

Hours later, Anna sits alone in the hole. A dark room with bare floorboards and dampness. No light can slip in, no warmth. She shivers wildly.

There will be no food and no drinks until the prophet decides she has been punished enough.

She tries to recall her life from before. She loved dusty books and learning. Her mother was always dreaming, always searching for the next big thing to believe in. The cult sunk their brainwashing hooks into her and life took a sharp turn into oblivion. A one-way trip to annihilation.

There were no relatives and no father to run away to, and now, she has no future either.

What is she but a thing to pleasure a man, a thing to breed like a racehorse or collection of shiny, branded cattle.

She recalls folklore and old stories, real ones with vivid meanings, tales of otherworldly queens with grace and power. Ancient history rich with divine goddesses. Warrior women. Stories that were stolen by man and changed, altered until nothing of truth remained. Wild women roaming thick woodlands, water nymphs, Medusa, Lilith, the one before Eve, the fierce woman refused to be controlled. The tales became about disempowerment. A way to blind a woman, a trick, circus mirrors to prevent reality from being seen.

Metaphorical pink ribbons are now forced upon the female of the species, dresses of lace and the hiding of flesh, lest the body tempts a man who has no control and has rot for a heart.

Blame. The nagging woman archetype, the complaining wife, all done for coercive control reasons. All done to cause shame.

Even at fifteen years old, she knows this. Fake superiority, she is bleeding at her core and like all women, is bleeding at her roots.

Yet all she can do is sit in a locked room and wait for a man to decide her fate, wait for the thing inside her to arrive, and rip her to shreds.

It will kill me.

Anna finds she doesn't mind. Existence is intolerable when she is not allowed ownership of her own body. Perhaps an afterlife will provide the equality she craves.

Change will not visit the miles of land the cult owns. It is a prison ground, a locked compound. Her shackles are invisible but still bind her tightly.

"Kill me," she tells her bulging stomach. "Kill . . . "

The door interrupts her pleas, it creaks and opens, and a figure stands in dark shadows.

"Who is it?" she whispers, afraid. If it's him, he will bring objects with which to hurt her. Vicious tools of conquest to torture her until she submits.

Submissive. She hates the word and finds it as repulsive as the cult collective, the hive mind of insanity.

"Shhh, I brought you a drink of water," a barely-there voice whispers.

Mary, one of the prophets' many wives. Polygamy is rife. The woman tiptoes over quietly and places a plastic glass in her hands. Anna drinks it greedily.

"I'll bring you another tomorrow if I can."

"No," Anna begs. "Please . . . help me now. There's something inside me and it's wrong. It hurts. I need a doctor. It's a parasite, a demon. I heard them chanting, it's all a lie. They have dark ritual ways. Bad magic."

"Magic doesn't exist and hush, it's a baby inside you, a child of the prophet."

"No, no, it isn't. Believe me, please. Help me get rid of it."

"I've told you, the problem is in your mind, not your belly. You speak of such terrible sins, Anna."

Mary snatches the glass and leaves, closing the door softly behind her. Darkness engulfs Anna. She welcomes the pitch black.

The thing inside her stomach stretches; it hurts so much that her breath leaves her.

However did it come to this? She went to school, she had friends, and her whole life was ahead of her.

She feels an abrupt warmth between her legs.

Anna half believes she has wet herself until the cold truth dawns. She knows what it is, what it means.

"Oh no, please no!" She cries in panic. A flash of pain so blinding hot strikes. She tries to move, tries to crawl to the door. White-hot agony tears her soul apart. Dizziness threatens to swallow her.

"Help!" she screams. She hates them all, every single one of them but now she needs assistance.

It's far too soon, it's too fast. The monster is coming. Now, she truly is bleeding at her core, her roots. A flood of crimson arrives, and black spots burst across her vision. Wave after wave of anguish, of terror, of hopelessness.

She feels herself weakening, spiraling down.

Nothing is in her control, not one thing. Her body attempts to assist her and tries to expel the demon from within. Her stomach quakes and undulates, she parts her legs and pushes.

She can't breathe, the pain is so bright her mind rejects awareness and shuts down.

Anna falls down into darkness and chaos.

She dreams she is a goddess, emerging from a pretty shell, ready with a bow and arrows to defeat her enemies.

❖ ❖ ❖

The door of the hole is gone when she awakes, not open, but missing entirely, only shards remain, mere splinters.

Thirst so great grips her; her mouth and body are parched. She tests her limbs and attempts to move. Light seeps in and she sees the ground around her. Blood and mucus, stains of horror, and what looks like eggshells, but simply can't be. Each sign of violence covers the strange symbols already etched onto the floor.

Anna cannot think in straight lines. Her mind is muddled and confused, quicksand in her brain. Her being is sore and tender, as wounded as her shattered heart.

In one brutal blow, she remembers.

Where is it?

They called it a baby, but she knew it was no such thing. Her words and warning landed on ears conditioned to ignore the female voice.

She crawls forward, eager to see, desperate for a drink and help.

It didn't kill me. I'm alive.

She cannot tell if she is pleased or disappointed. She reaches the staircase and shuffles up with all her energy.

An object blocks her path, a human body. Mary. Her pretty long dress has been shredded open, and her flesh has been sliced wide as easily as butter. White ribs are on display and glistening red organs.

Animal attack?

Lies and she knows it. Acid rises in her throat and burns, she swallows and crawls over the corpse, strangely indifferent.

In the small and simple kitchen, she hauls herself up and drinks several glasses of water.

The view out of the window stuns her. Her eyes see the crimes of a daylight massacre.

Bodies and body parts lie under the hot sun. She cannot tell who is who; the blood spilled is too severe. A figure in a white gown catches her eye, she recognizes the outfit, although the head of the corpse is missing.

Am I dreaming?

She pinches her skin and gasps at the sharp pain.

A tiny spark of joy erupts inside her. One of the elders is dead, the meanest, cruelest one with a soul of depravity. Her own mother too. She hangs, tangled in a barbed-wire fence designed to keep chickens inside its boundaries. Her face is intact; she looks horrified and surprised. Her stomach has been sliced open; intestines trail across the ground. Flies swarm, eager for a delicious feast.

Anna does not feel sad. She begins to smile. She stumbles outside, wondering if anyone is left alive.

No. A war occurred and the cult members were not the victors.

What happened here? Who did this?

A strange sound behind alerts her.

I birthed a monster after all.

She tried to warn them.

The thing from inside her belly sits casually on a fence post. It clings to the wood with narrow scaled legs and spitefully long talons. Vast wings of sleek black and gray color spread out behind it.

What is it?

It resembles a harpy from a Greek mythology book she once owned and thought beautiful, but that would be impossible. The face of it is just like her own and pretty in its own horrible way. Its upper chest is that of a woman, the rest is hidden by feathers and scales that glimmer in the sunlight.

Cold gray eyes reveal intelligence, brutality, and vengeance.

She stands, entranced by the majesty it holds. It is all power, all force. A personification of vanished aspirations, trauma, fear, and chaos.

Dark rituals gone awry and feminine rage created something new, or something old. The seed inside her chose a different path, a unique destination.

She, not it. Her.

Anna wonders if she will be the next one to fall victim to those lethal razor-like claws.

She falls to her knees, incomprehension and shock swarming her. The visions she sees have stained her eyelids with pure horror.

The disbelief is so fierce that she feels as if she has already left her body. She closes her eyes and braces for impact.

Let it be quick.

The creature does not strike her. Instead, it takes to the sky with beautiful grace, as big as an eagle, and circles smoothly.

She watches as she plummets down, sharper than a carefully aimed arrow.

The creature grips something, an object Anna cannot identify.

She screeches a wail of pure elegance and triumph before she flies over and drops what it is she was holding.

A gift, a trophy.

The object lands in front of Anna and rolls to a stop. The prophet, his head. Now, he bleeds at his core and bleeds everywhere.

She understands, the creature is showing her. Revenge has been carried out in her name, *for* her. The guilty faced judgment like never before, and it is them who were punished without mercy.

A prophet, who never saw what was to come. The irony.

Anna begins to laugh wildly and wonders if her mind has come undone. Mary was wrong; magic does exist after all.

She kicks the head far away from sight. In death, the ugly becomes grotesque.

She spends two days in an empty cabin, resting and healing as best she can. The creature is gone, she has not seen her, her magical kin. She too must yearn for a life of her own as a wild huntress. Freedom beckoned.

Anna understands, freedom calls for her too, a lure too compelling to ignore.

Her flesh, blood, bone, and spirit all belong to herself now. Fertility is hers to nurture or hers to end. She owns her own womb. She will not silence her own stories, she will not be bound by invisible chains.

She will not be a prisoner.

She makes her escape, her departure easy. No human eyes are left to watch the mechanical camera eyes.

She will find her own place in the world and help create a tidal wave of compassionate change.

She can be anyone.

She bleeds at her core, like all of us. Sinner, saint, kind, angry, child, mother, she is capable of everything and all.

No will of others will be placed upon her. No patriarchal rules or domination.

Anna will not submit. She will not be refused.

She will bleed at her roots no more and instead, will rise and stay rooted.

Feed Us
Zack Zagranis

First Trimester

"Fuck!"

Alex stared at the lines on the urine-soaked stick. She held the pregnancy test in a death grip as the word *positive* hit her like a ton of bricks. How could this happen? Alex had been on the pill since she was sixteen.

"FUCK!"

Alex slammed her fist into the metal partition with a loud *BANG*. The woman in the stall next to her inhaled sharply. Alex muttered a weak apology, but she didn't really give a shit if anyone heard her tantrum. She was pissed. Alex looked down at the two pink lines and frowned. She had read once that the pill was something like 99.7% effective, practically foolproof. The test had to be faulty. That was the only reasonable explanation.

Alex calmed herself and called Doctor Matthews. The rational thing would be to get confirmation before she started freaking out. Thanks to a last-minute cancellation, the doctor was able to squeeze her in for an exam later that day. Alex thanked him and let out a sigh of relief. She dropped the pregnancy test in the trash and headed back to work. On the way to her desk, Alex popped into the manager's office and told him she was going home early. All it took were the words *woman problems*, and he practically shoved her out of the building.

❖ ❖ ❖

Doctor Matthews only confirmed what Alex feared: she was pregnant. She started bawling her eyes out, and the doctor mistook her tears for ones of joy. He congratulated her, but Alex only cried harder. Her tears were borne of fear and anger, not happiness. Alex knew Doctor Matthews wouldn't understand how she felt, not that she could stop crying long enough to tell him. No man would understand.

Men were allowed to be scared of their babies. They could run away from their responsibilities only to return years later and be praised just for showing up. But women? Women weren't allowed to be scared. A woman had to greet pregnancy as a blessing; it was the unspoken rule. She had to embrace motherhood and let it become her sole identity; otherwise, she would be labeled a monster and branded with adjectives like *cold* and *selfish*.

Alex didn't consider herself cold just because her uterus didn't ache whenever she saw a woman with a baby. Supposedly, her biological clock had started ticking around thirty, but at thirty-three, Alex hadn't heard a single tick.

 She started to go through her options as soon as she left the doctor's office. There weren't many: keep it, give it up for adoption, or abort it. Alex was lucky to live in a state where number three was still an option. Probably the best option if she was being honest with herself. By the time she reached her car, she had made a decision. Tomorrow was Friday. If Alex took the day off, that would give her the weekend to recuperate from the procedure. That settled it. She would call out of work in the morning, drive to Planned Parenthood, and get an abortion.

Alex told her husband about their little bundle of sorrow that night over dinner. She couldn't wait to hear his reaction. She imagined it would be similar to hers, minus the pounding on the bathroom stall. Brad had always shared her lack of interest in starting a family. Alex wouldn't have married him if he hadn't.

Brad shocked her by casually suggesting they keep the baby. They had always agreed they valued their freedom too much to have children. Brad's sudden turnaround on the prospect of fatherhood left Alex feeling betrayed. First, her own body screwed her over, and now her partner was doing the same thing. Brad tried to convince Alex that she had maternal instincts buried somewhere inside her. He promised her that once the baby started growing, she would fall in love with it. Alex wasn't so sure. Every time she tried to picture a baby, she saw a clump of cells, dividing and growing like a tumor inside her womb. A cancerous parasite that would feed off of her very livelihood. She told Brad as much, but he pushed back. Alex was crazy; how could *his* offspring be a parasite? Brad begged and pleaded until Alex gave in and became just another wife ignoring her own needs to please her husband.

Alex lay in bed that night, searching her phone for pregnancy horror stories. Brad lay beside her, scrolling through baby names and gently caressing her belly. After reading about a particularly gruesome ectopic pregnancy, Alex put her phone down in revulsion. Brad rolled over and immediately passed out. Alex watched her husband sleep, disgusted by the newfound glow surrounding his face. Brad told her at dinner that he wanted a child to carry on his genes and leave behind some kind of legacy. The usual male bullshit. Alex would do all the work, and the final product would carry *his* name.

Alex wished she felt anything other than disgust for the tiny cluster of cells growing inside her, but she would be lying if she said she did. She just couldn't muster up much affection for something the size of a grain of rice. Alex worried that she was broken. She stared at the ceiling listening to Brad snoring beside her, oblivious to her internal turmoil. Eventually, Alex's brain quieted down, and she fell into a restless slumber of her own.

"Feed us!"

Alex tried to move, but the straps were too tight. A doctor stood over her, his face covered in shadow. Alex heard the high-pitched whine of a power tool and looked around in a panic. The doctor raised a circular saw and held it threateningly above her abdomen. The saw came down, and Alex screamed as the blade bit into her stomach. The hungry teeth chewed up her flesh, sending chunks of fat and muscle flying in all directions. Blood shot out of the wound like a crimson geyser. The doctor reached his hand into Alex's stomach and pulled out a fetus covered in mucous, lesions, and open sores. Partially formed limbs grew randomly all over its malformed body. Its black, lifeless doll eyes stared at Alex as one of the sores opened wide enough to speak.

"Feed us!" the creature rasped.

Alex woke up drenched in sweat. She thought it was blood until she looked around her decidedly gore-free bed. She sighed. It must have been a dream. Alex dragged herself out of bed and started her morning routine. By the time she finished her shower, the nightmare had already faded from her mind, replaced with a tenuous optimism. Today was a new day, and even though Alex didn't feel an emotional connection to her baby yet, she was determined to fake it until she did. Alex dressed and went downstairs to make herself a cup of coffee before work. Brad met her at the bottom of the stairs with a Dunkin' Donuts cup. He held it out to Alex like a peace offering. She smiled. For a moment,

Alex allowed herself to believe that this whole ordeal might not be that bad. The moment was ruined as soon as she took a sip of her coffee. Brad had gotten her decaf because it was *better for the baby*.

Maybe I should make that trip to the clinic, after all, Alex thought.

❖ ❖ ❖

Alex knew something was wrong when she weighed herself the night before her first check-up and saw she had *lost* weight. It was only a couple of pounds, but still, it was a couple of pounds in the *wrong* direction. She mentioned her concern to Brad, who just shrugged.

"Would you rather get fat?"

The next day, Alex told Doctor Matthews about her weight loss.

"It's no cause for alarm," he assured her. "There are many things that can cause a woman to shed a few pounds at the start of her pregnancy. Like morning sickness or maybe a sudden urge to eat healthier?"

Alex shook her head. She hadn't thrown up once. On the contrary, her appetite had been ravenous. And she wasn't watching what she ate either. Besides giving up caffeine to appease Brad, she hadn't made any changes to her diet. Doctor Matthews still didn't think it was anything to worry about and chalked it up to anxiety. He put a hand on Alex's shoulder and squeezed it lightly.

"Trust me, soon you'll be gaining weight like there's no tomorrow."

Second Trimester

One morning near the beginning of her second trimester, Alex was eating scrambled eggs when she felt a sharp pain in her mouth. She looked down and saw something white sitting in a pool of blood next to her eggs. Alex poked her tongue around and confirmed what she already suspected: her front tooth was missing. In a panic, she ran to the bathroom.

Alex stared at the bloody gap in her mouth. Two more teeth quivered slightly before falling into the sink. Alex closed her eyes and thought back to when she was hiking as a child and found a rotting animal carcass full of maggots. She could still see the fur writhing as they fought over the meat left on the bones. Alex imagined it was her skin stretched over the bones with the fetus squirming underneath and started gagging. The gagging turned into a breathless wailing as she opened her eyes and saw her mouth grotesquely reflected back at her.

Her baby was like those maggots hiding under her flesh and devouring her insides. It feasted on her calcium, drained her of iron, and consumed everything. The fetus would grow big and strong, and Alex would become an empty husk of a woman.

Alex stared at the cursed image in the mirror. Flecks of blood and saliva sprayed the mirror when she breathed. Soon yellowish pus started oozing from the holes in her gums.

Alex stood in shock, watching as one tiny drop after another flew from her mouth as she stood there breathing heavily. When the shock finally wore off, Alex cleaned herself up and called in sick to work. She didn't consider herself a vain person, but she refused to leave the house with three of her *adult* teeth missing. Alex crawled back into bed and waited for Brad to get home. Six o'clock came, and Alex met her husband at the door, holding the three teeth in the palm of her hand.

Brad's first question was "What did you do?"

Not, "*What happened?*"

Not, "*Are you okay?*"

But an immediate accusation that Alex was somehow responsible for the new gaps in her smile. He started berating her for not taking enough prenatal vitamins and whatever other pregnancy buzzwords he had picked up. When Alex tried to tell her husband it was the baby's fault, she was met with condescension. Brad told her it was just hormones messing up her head.

He could think what he wanted, but Alex knew her body better than anyone else, and no one would convince her otherwise. Brad insisted on taking charge of her health for the remainder of the pregnancy. Alex didn't have the energy to argue, so she went along with Brad's Alpha Male Posturing for the time being.

Brad kept his promise and accompanied Alex to her next check-up. From the moment they entered the examination room Doctor Matthews directed all of the questions he would typically ask her toward Brad.

"How is she eating?"

"Is she taking her vitamins?"

"You're not letting her spend too much time on her feet, are you?"

Alex felt utterly invisible. She stepped into the bathroom to change into an examination gown and left Brad to tell Doctor Matthews about her teeth. Alex came out in time to hear the doctor tell Brad that a hormone increase had temporarily loosened the tissue in her gums.

"I knew it had something to do with hormones!" Brad said proudly.

Alex rolled her eyes as she climbed onto the examination table.

Brad told Doctor Matthews about his wife's crazy idea that the baby was eating her from the inside. The two men chuckled as Alex nervously poked her tongue around, searching for any more loose teeth. Not feeling any wiggles, Alex let out a sigh of relief. Brad assumed the sigh was directed at him and immediately got defensive. He accused Alex of not being able to take a joke. She sat there quietly and didn't respond. Alex just wanted to get out of her examination gown and into something where her ass wasn't hanging out.

Doctor Matthews finally acknowledged Alex's presence. He put on a more professional demeanor as he explained that it was common for expecting mothers to sometimes imagine their baby as a parasite. Doctor Matthews told Alex not to be ashamed for feeling that way and assured her that the baby wasn't *really* leeching the calcium from her bones and teeth. Alex could have imagined it, but she thought she saw the doctor wink at Brad as he said the last part.

The only thing that did concern Doctor Matthews was Alex's weight. She wasn't gaining much and what little weight she did gain was just the baby getting larger. The doctor asked Alex if she was eating enough, and she giggled uncomfortably. Alex had, in fact, been eating *more* than enough. Subs, chips, brownies—nothing seemed to satisfy the insatiable hunger gnawing at the pit of her stomach.

Alex would gorge herself on an entire sleeve of Oreos during her lunch break and be hungry again an hour later. She knew where the food was going. *It* was taking everything, every last morsel. Alex remembered the voice from her dream, "*Feed Us!*" and started giggling again, louder this time.

The doctor and Brad appeared uneasy and excused themselves to talk privately outside the examination room. Alex couldn't hear them, but she knew what they were talking about. She could imagine them using words like *hysterical* and talking about her like some Victorian housewife suffering from the vapors. Alex imagined them fitting her with a straitjacket and dragging her kicking and screaming down the corridor of a sanitarium. The two men returned from their secret huddle. Doctor Matthews told Alex they were finished, and she could change back into her clothes.

"I want an abortion." Alex's voice was a little shaky, but the men understood her just fine. "As soon as possible. I want this thing out of me."

"What?" Brad's face sunk. "But it's too late. We already said we were keeping it!"

"Bullshit." Alex got down from the examination table and stood toe to toe with her husband. "I'm allowed to change my mind. I don't feel safe anymore." She turned to Doctor Matthews for support but found none. Unsurprisingly, he sided with Brad.

"Alex, you've already come this far. You don't want to have an abortion now." He gestured to Brad, "You and your husband made a decision together. It would be selfish for you to change your mind now."

"If you won't schedule it, I'll go to Planned Parenthood," Alex said defiantly. "I don't care. I just want this *thing* out of me. My teeth are falling out, for fuck's sake, I don't want to wait around for something worse to happen."

Brad started sobbing into the crook of his arm. Doctor Matthews looked at Alex like she was an inhuman monster. Alex looked down at the floor. She was tired, so tired of everything. On top of that, she was starving *again*.

"I just want to go home," Alex said softly.

On the drive home, Brad suggested that Alex stay home for the remainder of her pregnancy. He was concerned for Alex's well-being and thought that maybe if she took some time off, she wouldn't be so stressed.

You just want me to stop throwing around the A word, Alex thought. She knew it was the baby's survival that drove Brad's decision to cut their weekly income in half, not hers.

Alex protested. This was not how marriage was supposed to be, at least not for her. Alex refused to end up like her mother, staying at home, catering to the whims of four children and a husband so needy he might as well be child number five. She had already compromised by agreeing to carry this thing inside her for nine months; she would not give up her career, too. Brad swore it was only until the baby was born, but Alex knew better. If she caved now, next time Brad would try to talk her into staying home until the kid was in school full time.

Brad kept at it until he wore her down. Alex just didn't have the strength to fight back. She called work the next day and took an extended leave of absence.

Third Trimester

Things only got worse in the third trimester. One day, Alex was in the shower washing her hair when she heard a sound like cooked spaghetti hitting a linoleum floor. She looked down to see a long brown clump of hair—still covered in shampoo suds—lying at her feet. Alex stopped moving her hands through her hair, fearing what else might fall out, and quickly put her head under the water to rinse. As the water cascaded down around her head, Alex thought she heard the sound of more hair hitting the tub. Alex was afraid to pull her head out from under the water and look down. Instead, she reached up and felt her scalp. It was unsettlingly smooth beneath her fingertips. Alex opened her eyes to look, and a scream of horror escaped her throat.

Long soapy clumps of brown hair covered the floor of her bathtub. Some of it started to clog the drain, causing the water to rise. The ropey strands wove their way around her ankles like snakes. Alex leapt from the tub, accidentally ripping down the shower curtain. She turned off the water before it could drench everything outside and slumped down on the toilet. Alex gazed down at her belly and cursed the thing inside. She watched her skin bulge with disgust as the baby moved.

It had been six months, give or take, and Alex still had no affection for the unwanted guest in her womb. She felt contempt, resentment, anger, all the emotions a good mother should never feel toward her baby, but not love.

Alex started to cry. She ran her tongue around the dental appliance she had begun wearing to fill in the gaps where her teeth had fallen out. Alex looked at her arms. They were so thin she could wrap her hand around her wrist, and her fingers would touch. Her ribs were visible above her swollen belly. Her stomach increased in size as the rest of her body wasted away. She was pregnant with a leech.

Alex stood up and shuffled over to the sink. She looked up at the bathroom mirror and gasped. Her head was completely bald except for a few sparse patches. The remaining wisps of hair were brittle and straw-like, as if something had sucked out all of the vitality through her follicles. *Feed us!* Alex started laughing uncontrollably.

Brad came home and found Alex lying naked on the bathroom floor. She looked up at him and started laughing again. The hair floating in the tub caused Brad to retch. He turned away, and something red caught his eye. Before collapsing to the bathroom floor, Alex had scrawled *Eat of my flesh, drink of my blood* on the mirror with a tube of red lipstick.

Brad gently lifted Alex up and carried her to the bedroom. He was startled by how light she was. His hand brushed against Alex's protruding ribs, and he shuddered. Brad hadn't paid attention to any part of Alex's body other than her belly for months. He had been entirely oblivious to how thin she was getting. Brad helped Alex into her pajamas and tucked her into bed. Once she was settled in, he began cleaning the bathroom.

Brad brought his wife dinner in bed but refused to make eye contact with her. Alex tried to thank him, to start a conversation, but he left the bedroom without saying a word. Her eyes filled with tears. Alex was losing any connection she'd ever had with her husband. Brad didn't talk to her anymore unless it was about the baby, and they hadn't had sex since before she got pregnant. The only part of her body he would touch was her belly. When Brad looked at her, Alex wondered if he saw a toothless, hairless mutant or some paragon of motherhood. A goddess sitting on a pedestal above the filthy needs of the flesh and bloated with his divine seed. Maybe a bit of both. All Alex knew was that Brad no longer saw her as a woman, the one thing she *wanted* him to see.

Eventually, her ravenous appetite overtook her sadness, and she wolfed down her dinner. With her hunger satisfied, she climbed out of bed and walked carefully to her dresser. Alex winced as she bent down to open her bottom drawer, exposing her modest lingerie collection. Alex pulled out Brad's favorite Teddy and matching panties and laid them on the bed. Before checking her reflection in the bedroom mirror, she changed out of her pajamas and into her (hopefully) seductive lingerie. The teddy hung a little loose but all things considered, it didn't look too bad. The weight loss had given her a waifish figure, and she had cheekbones for days. Alex grabbed a silk scarf and wrapped it around her newly bald head. She put on makeup for the first time since she stopped working, and the final result wasn't half bad. Alex felt sexy for the first time in months.

Alex hoped a night of intimacy might bring her and Brad closer. She lay down on the bed provocatively and called for Brad. Alex bit her lip coyly and waited to hear his footsteps approaching. The moment Brad set foot in the bedroom, Alex leapt from the bed and began kissing him, but he just stood perfectly still with his hands at his sides. Alex pulled away and stared up at her husband's face. She saw no passion there whatsoever.

Alex blamed her barren gums and bald head for Brad's lack of interest, but he insisted it was her frail body that kept him away.

"Something could break."

"Please," Alex pleaded, wrongfully assuming it was her Brad was worried about. "I'll be fine. We can take it slow."

"But what if we hurt the baby?"

So that was what he saw her as, packaging. To Brad, she was an eggshell and nothing more.

Alex was crushed. She swung her fists against Brad's chest, but she had become so weak there was no force behind her blows. Alex screamed at Brad to get out through fat, blubbery tears. He left without a word. That night Alex couldn't sleep. She kept thinking about the greedy *thing* growing inside of her. The gluttonous parasite had started feeding off of Brad, too. It had sucked out all of her husband's compassion and tenderness, bloating itself like a tick. Now it was moving on to his libido, gorging itself on Brad's virility. Alex couldn't wait to get this cancer cut out of her, and she didn't feel the least bit guilty about it.

Halfway through her third trimester, Alex got up in the middle of the night to use the bathroom and collapsed halfway there. Brad heard the commotion and jumped out of bed to see what was wrong. He found Alex on the floor in a puddle of urine, unable to get up. Brad lifted her off the floor and started cleaning her up. When he was done, he dressed Alex in clean clothes and rushed her to the hospital.

The ER doctor explained to Alex that her thigh and calf muscles had atrophied to the point where the baby's weight had become too much for her weakened legs to support.

"I have to be honest. I've only seen this once before in a woman starving herself to stay thin during her pregnancy."

Before the doctor could accuse Alex of doing the same, she told him everything she had been eating daily. He gave her an incredulous chuckle and insisted that she would be much heavier if she took in the number of calories she claimed. He looked at Brad to corroborate her claims, but Brad just shrugged and said that he worked too much to keep track of what food Alex was or wasn't eating.

"It's the baby!" Alex shouted at the doctor. "It's a parasite! It's taking all the food and giving me a tiny bit, just enough to keep me alive."

Alex could see in the doctor's eyes that he thought she was crazy. He pulled Brad aside and started discussing Alex as if she weren't there. Maybe he thought she couldn't hear him, but Alex thought it more likely that he just didn't care. She made out the words *danger to herself* and *constant vigilance*. Alex imagined Brad would have to take time off from work to babysit her. Something he would probably resent Alex for. The doctor told Brad to keep his wife in bed until the baby came, which he happily agreed to. Bed rest would keep Alex from getting into any more trouble. He had been unable to clean the lipstick completely off the bathroom mirror, and every time he washed his hands, he saw the ghost of his wife's words and shuddered.

When they got home, Brad carried Alex up the stairs like a sleeping child and gently tucked her into bed. Brad looked down at his wife's protruding cheekbones and her smooth head. He took out her dental appliance—thin strands of saliva still connecting it to her gums—and inspected her barren mouth.

"I love you, you know . . . "

Alex looked into Brad's eyes and saw only pity and blame. He looked at her as one might look down at a drug addict rotting in the gutter.

"I know," Alex whispered. But she didn't know, not anymore.

Over the next month, Alex left her bed only to go to the bathroom or see the doctor. The rest of her time was spent weaving in and out of sleep. She looked horrendous. Her eyes had sunken into her head, and the rest of her teeth had fallen out, giving her a freakish smile. Her body had become gaunt and fragile, no more than a bag of bones.

When Alex slept, she dreamt of the thing inside her clawing slowly at the walls of her uterus, biding its time until it was strong enough to break out of its fleshy prison. The nightmare fetus had mutated into a cancerous abomination covered in tumors. Its lifeless black eyes had been replaced with milky orbs that leaked something wet and yellow. Instead of a mouth, there was a ragged gash as if the creature started to split itself in half but thought better of it. The dreams always ended with a wet gurgle of a voice choking out the words, "Feed us!"

Sometimes the baby would move around, and Alex could see her distended abdomen twist and contort. Her belly pulsated grotesquely with every breath the baby took. There was no more fat on her body, and when the baby stretched, Alex could see individual fingers and toes trying to poke through her skin.

Doctor Matthews had insisted on a c-section, believing Alex was too weak to survive a natural birth. The morning it was scheduled, Alex woke up in the worst pain of her life. The baby wanted out and wasn't shy about letting her know. She felt a tug on her insides like someone was trying to pull her guts out through her genitals. She screamed for Brad, and he came running. He started to lift Alex off the bed, and she spewed hot bile all over him. A pool of blood spread between her legs. Brad laid her back down and called 911. He explained the situation to the dispatcher, and she started to talk him through the delivery.

Alex started convulsing as the fetus attempted to drag itself out of her body. The baby tried to push through her emaciated figure, dislocating her hips with a loud pop. Brad turned around and saw his wife's legs bent at an impossible angle. The thing struggled to free itself, pushing a small piece of intestine out through Alex's anus. Brad saw the slimy rope sticking out of his wife's backside and vomited.

The grotesque sound of tearing skin filled the air as the baby thrashed around hard enough to displace several of Alex's organs. One of Alex's lungs collapsed, and her vision filled with spots as she struggled to breathe. Brad stared at the horror show in disbelief, vomit still dripping from his lower lip. The shrill cry of a newborn filled the air as Alex started to split open from her groin to her sternum. Lying there, surrounded by entrails and covered in blood, was the most beautiful thing Brad had ever seen. It was a baby, *his* baby. Brad carefully reached into Alex's open abdominal cavity and picked up his child. The baby wailed as Brad gently stroked its hair and cooed softly. He placed the child gently on Alex's chest. She weakly wrapped her arms around the infant as her heart struggled to pump blood to her exposed innards.

"It's a boy!" Alex smiled weakly as she said her last words: "I think he's hungry."

ALL FALL DOWN
Angela Sylvaine

Lovely laughing girl blooms,
nourished by the scent of fresh cut grass
as she dances with dandelions in the sun

Boys watch her shimmering halo
coming to claim curls as keepsakes,
crushing flower friends
whose downy heads flee on the breeze

Raw girl seeks comfort but finds none
They say boys hurt what they like
and good girls are grateful

Boys advance again,
feet crunching fallen leaves
releasing decay's rotten perfume
Pruned and choking on thank you's
gratitude scrapes her throat raw

Wilted girl begs the watchers
for help but they only blame,
faulting the temptress who snares
and leaves none for those longing
to be destroyed by desire

Tormented girl shakes, bitten by frost
as stalkers strike to tear at thinned tresses
She sobs when watchers follow
snatching strands to leave her bare
scalp crying copper

Destroyed girl seethes,
pain feeding rising wrath
as curses slither from her scaled tongue,
commanding silken trophies
to twine wrists and arms
climb and circle bared throats
stuff shrieking mouths
until all fall down around her
breathless bodies turning stony
within their spoiled shrouds

The Rabbits that Make Us Wolves
Bri Crozier

The rabbits never condemn the wolves for the things they do, as the clover fields have never condemned the rabbits. A rabbit understands what she is, and a wolf understands what she is, and the clover fields understand what they are. It will hurt, as all things do, but that is the nature of living. The rabbit knows what will become of her body and she thanks the universe for letting her live amongst it. And the wolf thanks the rabbit for becoming a meal. No part of this exchange is fool enough to doubt their place in it. No part is fool enough to think they are owed any more than what they have wrought. The rabbit's life is as much a gift to the wolf as it is to the rabbit.

    —Rabbit Funeral Prayer

Bristle brush danced against the rabbit's fur as she lay, tucked tidy under the bramble. This is the way of rabbits, to hide downwind so the rabbit smell does not carry far. How lucky she was to have listened in time. The moment she had smelled the wolf upwind, she had dashed under the thicket, trembling. She could smell the wolf long before the wolf would ever smell her, she knew, but that in itself was a backhanded blessing.

As a kit, she was always called a fool, straying far too close to the wolves. She couldn't help it; something in her instincts misfired. How could she feel fear when their musky smell and rounded voices were so enticing, the glint of their eye as transfixing as the sharpness of their teeth? There was a pull like a snare at her ankle that made her stay, begging for just another moment close to them. She could quell it now, pull back mentally, unlike the physical yanks in her youth. Her mother's sharp whisper still rang through her head whenever she was caught by the unmistakable smell of the wolves. 'A rabbit knows what she is. That is the way of rabbits.' In respect of her mother, she had pushed that hunger down, swallowed so deep and away that it lived with the emptiness that flowers left in her stomach, no meal quite enough to satiate her. She buried it down still, with the wrongness of her body, the voice that lived in her mind and not her throat. She buried these like a collapsed den, so it might never resurface. But that is never how these things work. She felt it, too often, rise up like burning bile every time she was caught by the glint of wolf eyes at twilight.

She had yet to see or hear the wolf, but the smell grew strong, along with the memories she could never quite grasp. It was like she remembered having known it once, but not anymore. When she tried to catch it now, it would melt away as she reached for it, pond frost on a spring morning with her as the sun. It was gone too quick to understand. Desperate to ignore it, the rabbit bit down on her own tongue, tasting the blood well in her mouth. Her stomach ached at the taste of it. And it was a fruitless venture anyway; the snare was triggered the moment the wolf stepped into view.

Seeing it felt like breaking the surface as you drowned. The wolf was lithe and lean, her fur nearly golden in its delicacy. Pale blonde rippling across long-limbed muscles, muddled by the leaf-filtered light. The wolf had an air of elegance, of confidence in her body the rabbit could never even begin to comprehend. Head raised and ears twitching in anticipation, the rabbit watched as the wolf walked, gentle as sunlight, through the grass glade. All the rabbit could do was wonder how a wolf could ever be so fair.

Ducking her head, the wolf sniffed at the ground, parting the tall grasses with a lazy grace. By now, the rabbit knew the wolf could smell her in the bramble. It set her heart racing for all the wrong reasons. Given the wolf's leisurely pace, the rabbit doubted her location was completely revealed to the wolf, giving ample opportunity for the thrilling game of hide and seek. The rabbit felt no fear, only intrigue as she stayed frozen stiff, waiting for the feeling to change into what it should be. But it never did. Instead, the rabbit watched as the wolf gave up her hunt, a twinge of disappointment making the fur on her back twitch. From there, the wolf sat back on her haunches, lifted her head to the sky, and sang.

Rabbits do not sing. At least, not in the way of wolves. They are a quiet folk who chitter and chew, and scream when need be. But they do not sing. The song as a concept alone sent the rabbit shaking, shivers of cold delight running down her spine like rivulets of rain. Now would be the time to run, when the wolf wouldn't hear the grass parting over the sound of her own voice. Now would be the time to feel fear. The rabbit wished she felt fear. It would have been easier than this, but all she felt was an empty hearted need, so close to being fulfilled. She listened to the wolf song, felt it rise up in her throat, choking her on notes she could not sing, words she could not form. The song was not words to her, only a cry, but she could understand, on some level, it was meant for her in a way it should never be for a rabbit.

The wolf ended her singing, standing to shake off the stillness. The rabbit knew she was about to leave, couldn't stand the thought of the empty stomach feeling the song left her with. She needed the wolf to stay even if it meant she would risk filling something else's stomach instead of her own. Before she could think about what she was doing, the rabbit called out, "Wolf! Wolf! What does your song mean?"

The golden wolf startled, turning with a snarl. Though no one was obviously behind her, she stayed cautious, hunched as she paced around the edge of the glade. "Who's there?"

Embarrassed, the rabbit replied, "A—a wolf."

The wolf barked a disbelieving laugh, and the rabbit felt like an idiot. "Is that so? Show yourself. Why would you hide from me? And why would you need to ask what I sing? What wolf wouldn't know?"

"Won't you just play along? Humor me, in good fun."

The wolf paused, eyes scanning the bramble before her snarl warmed into a devilish smile. "If I must." The wolf grew closer, her nose to the dirt, with the rabbit smell caught in the wind once again. "It's a song for other wolves. A call and response, I suppose."

"What is the song for?" The rabbit's heart beat faster, ears twitching against the blackberry thorns.

The wolf's ears twitched in turn, as she spoke next. "Partnership. If another wolf knows my song, then we are meant to be." The wolf crouched down, then, nose to nose with the rabbit, her great, golden eyes bright as the sun, bigger than the rabbit's paw. Her smiling teeth white as a warning. "Do you know my song, little rabbit?"

The rabbit's courage waned, but the wanting feeling didn't. "I don't know. What does it mean if I do?"

The wolf snorted, standing up from the brush. She turned to leave, calling back as she walked, "I don't know either, but you've entertained me. I'll leave you be. Humor you, *in good fun*." She paused then at the tree line, looking back over her shoulder. "Just for tonight, little rabbit."

And with that, the wolf darted past the underbrush and out of sight.

The rabbit was left floundering, letting out the breath she didn't know she was holding. Had that been an invitation? A request? *Partnership*? Could that even happen? She had heard tales of creatures becoming other creatures, but those were whispers, things no one spoke of in daylight or good company. But. Something about the golden wolf called to the rabbit, begging to break the cycle of wanting and waiting. It was time to act, and the rabbit knew just where to go.

❖ ❖ ❖

The rabbit wasn't sure what hit her first, the smell of the dogwood or the discordant song. She knew it was the only place to get the answer she needed, but it made it no more pleasant. She wrinkled her nose at the rotten smell; how the songbirds could stand it she would never know. She continued on, holding her breath as best she could until she reached the roots of the tree, and felt her lungs might burst. She looked up into a tree more bird than branch. Thousands of them bounced from limb to limb, chirping their stories to each other. Every bird held a story in song, sharing bits between each, so no story is lost if one falls. If anyone knew how the rabbit could join the wolves, it would be the songbirds of the old dogwood.

The rabbit let out her breath in a scream, breathing through the smell as she shouted up into the tree, "How do I become a wolf?"

The birds did not pause their chatter, but it changed. In place of the prior cacophony, was now harmony, and from a thousand voice choir came an answer. "To change what you are is not a decision taken lightly. To be a rabbit and to know the taste of rabbit flesh. If you take this path, the secrets of rabbits will never leave you, but you will not be a rabbit. You will become something in between, unless accepted as one or the other. To take this path, you must be claimed by the wolves, but the wolves will never claim you as their own. You will be left a thing in-between, an abomination to both wolves and rabbits."

The rabbit did her best to keep the annoyance out of her voice as she spoke, even as ever. "The rabbits have never condemned the wolves for what they are. And I have never been fully welcomed by the rabbits. I have never *been* a rabbit. Tell me how to become what I am. Please! Let me embrace it. You know this, you know what I am."

Her voice broke at the end, the desperation too much for her small, wrong voice.

The songbirds did not hesitate to answer. "We will not let you live to regret this. We will not give you the path to change. You are a rabbit, and you know this. We will not help you."

The voices returned then to chaos; the audience adjourned as the rabbit screamed in fury. It isn't their decision. It's not their fate. It's hers. Can't they see that? Can't they feel what she is, how she does? If they know so much, surely, they can know this, surely, they can see this. She called out to them, again, and again, and again, begging for them to acknowledge, to see, to listen. But they did not. The songbirds remained steadfast in their decision, leaving the rabbit with nothing but the smell of the tree and the sting of the songbird voices in her ear.

Her heart hardened then, as she understood that she would see no more council from the birds. Fine, then. She would show them just how much of a wolf she was. If they would not answer, she would claim it herself. In the cool voice of wolves, she spoke. "I know what I am. Let me prove it to you."

The rabbit did not let herself second guess her decision. She pressed down hard on her back feet, shooting up into the tree. The bottom branches hung low, overburdened with the weight of the songbirds, and she caught one in her mouth, pulling it back down to the roots with her, plucked like overripe fruit from a tree. The red juice filled her mouth as before, stomach growling in an impossible hunger, as the little songbird's heart beat hard and fast against her tongue. What the birds know, the rabbit understood, was kept in the flesh.

With a mouth never made for it, the rabbit ate. The hollow bird bones crunched under her teeth, marrow filling her mouth with a bitter, savory paste; feathers melting on her tongue like sugar lace. It was a messy fruit, coating her fur and face in purge, until the stench of it overpowered even the smell of the dogwood. Bite after bite she tore with her teeth, teeth made for flowers and brush now turned on ligament that snapped with a pull, rending skin from muscle. It was a wiry meat, full of gristle that scratched at her throat as it flowed down with each aching swallow. The bird never died as she enveloped it, not even when she crushed its heart with her lips, and drank.

In each bite, she could hear in her head what the songbird chorus refused to reveal.

Learn the stories of the wolves and you may grow fangs. Sing the songs of the wolves and you will grow claws. Speak the words only wolves may know and your eyes will glow like the sun. If your heart claims them, you will become a thing in between. If the wolves call you home, you will become the wolf they have always known you to be. If they do not, you will become a creature trapped in fractured understanding.

As the rabbit finished eating, she felt her body begin to change with what she had learned. Her teeth shifted in her mouth, the ache sharp as new teeth cut her gums, jaw cracking and rearranging with canine growth where rabbit molars once were. They were the wrong shape for her mouth, tearing at her cheeks and lips, filling her mouth with a new mix of bird blood and her own. Transformation already begun, and not wishing to wait for the songbirds to retaliate, the rabbit ran to where she now knew the wolves would be waiting.

The hill was crowded when the rabbit thing arrived, teeth having cut through full, pushing loose the old rabbit incisors. Her jaw still ached as she ducked under the tree line. She watched as the wolves began to gather, swarming on the hill like ants as the sun set, casting them in a faint golden glow. The rabbit remained silent as the wolves yipped and cried out their warm-up scales. Nervous, the rabbit's eyes darted from wolf to wolf, as their bodies melded together in the distance. She wanted to see the golden wolf, the one who started all of this, but she was nowhere in sight, lost in the sea of wolf forms.

The rabbit waited, gums still bleeding to the sound of the wolves murmuring and humming in impatience. As the rabbit still searched for her golden wolf, the wolves fell into a hush. Before the rabbit could fully understand the sudden silence, they all began to sing. It was a choir of howls, together in droning bass and melody on top, every wolf knowing their place in the symphony. The rabbit felt herself become whole as she listened, throat aching in the wrong shape, needing to join in a harmony she could hear, rising up her throat and choking her again on a voice that could not sing. But try she did, anyway.

The rabbit's voice was a scream to start, a shrill shriek of a creature caught in a fence, but it began to take new shape with the rabbit's body. Bones and fat shifting, ears shrinking and sharpening. Her jaw broke itself once more, reforming to better fit her new teeth, nose elongating into a pointed snout as her eyes moved from the side to front of her face, swift vertigo hitting the new creature as she tried to stay standing, had to keep singing. She had been huddled first, doubled over in pain when her body bowed, spine snapping straight and tail pulling away, fur gaining volume and density, but still somehow too downy for a wolf. Her legs burned and stretched, split side growing pains as they shot up too quickly, ankles and knees, and elbows breaking themselves into the right formation. The creature screamed the song still, as it understood it must, until vocal cords thickened into place and the scream became melody. It was painful, agonizing, but oh, it was delicious. It was euphoria, to feel her body change in this way, to feel long limbed and lithe. In the end, the creature hoped, it would be worth it.

The first song came to a close and in the brush was no longer a rabbit, but a wolf, with downy rabbit-colored fur. Her chest heaved with the labor of rebirth, still aching bone deep. After a moment of rest and to catch her new lungs' breath, she stood, delicate, on freshly thinned legs. Unsure of how best to use them yet, she took a testing step, stabbing sharp the feeling of paw pad on rocks, a challenge to overcome in her proper body. She knew, though, she would come to understand all her body's new quirks, as she quickly took to steps instead of hops. She took another, learning quickly how the legs worked in contrast, and keeping the momentum to fall into the rhythm of movement, however clumsy to start. Each step was hers, more so than any step she had ever taken prior, and she grinned her new wolfish grin, making her grin even more at the feel of it. It burned, each movement with an ache that stayed deep in her bones, but she didn't care. This was right. It was finally right.

She danced to the top of the hill where the other wolves were, running in clumsy circles around the pack, too full of ecstasy to notice their hackles raise and faces twist into snarls.

"Who are you?" one growled, ears back and teeth wet and shining.

The new wolf ducked her head, ears back in sheepish apology. She did not fully know the language and customs of the wolves, even as so much of it came to her naturally. With as much reverence as she could muster (though she could not truly hide her joy) she spoke in her young, round voice. "I'm a wolf! A wolf! Can't you see? I'm just a bit late." She almost laughed as the words bubbled out on this new voice. Her voice.

Another wolf circled her, sniffing at her downy fur, "You don't smell like a wolf. You smell like a rabbit."

"I've just eaten." She did not lie. Rabbit's blood still lingered on her teeth.

"You sound like a rabbit."

The new wolf began to feel desperate. She hadn't expected them to doubt her in this way. "I'm just young, that's all. My voice is still soft." Her enthusiasm fell away, letting the true ache of her bones hit her hard, making itself known. It was excruciating. She hoped to hurry this along, so she could rest in her new home. "Ask the golden wolf, she knows me. She knows who I am, ask her!"

The wolves shared side-eyed glances, more of them moving to surround her now, blocking any kind of escape. But it was fine, surely. Once the golden wolf claimed her, it would be fine. And besides, she couldn't run anyway, not now. Not with the ache in her spine and tremble in her legs. She wouldn't have the strength to fight them. The new wolf glances through the ranks, hopeful and searching for her golden wolf, waiting to see that intoxicating grin. *Look what I've done! I've done it! I'm here, just for you!* she wanted to say to the golden wolf when she saw that smile, imagining how they all would laugh and embrace her.

But she was not met with a grin when her gaze finally fell on that familiar face. Instead, she was greeted with stone-faced recognition and narrowed eyes. The golden wolf's ear twitched as she walked forward, calm and collected as she had been in the glade. The new wolf pleaded with tender eyes.

"Please. You know me, you know who I am. Please claim me, please tell them."

The golden wolf made no move to speak, only sitting on her haunches and towering over the tender wolf, who only now realized how small she was.

She looked up at the golden wolf, breath quickening as her hopes died and the pain rose up. "Please."

The golden wolf finally spoke. "I've never seen this creature before. I met a rabbit earlier, who smells the same as this thing, who sounded the same as this thing. I told it I would let it be, for the night. But maybe I have changed my mind, if it thinks itself to be a wolf."

The creature's heart dropped and so did its legs, giving out from below. The ache in them had become unbearable, unable to hold up their own weight, and the creature cried out as its bones began to tangle and break loose. The thing that was no more a wolf nor rabbit felt its mouth begin to rearrange, and through broken bone, gurgling on blood and spit as teeth cut out, it whimpered, once again a desperate, "*Please.*"

The golden wolf stepped back in disgust, the other wolves following suit, hackles raised in defense and distaste. The golden wolf snarled, teeth white and ready to finish it off if it didn't bleed itself to death. Her voice was low, a spiteful growl when she gave her reply. "I don't know what that thing is. But it is certainly not a wolf."

The creature, near nothing now, not wolf or rabbit, screamed as its spine curled in, vertebrae grinding against each other, fur falling out in clumps and leaving raw, oozing flesh behind. Its head hit the ground as it wept, before the golden wolf bore down, lunging for the source of the wailing. The creature felt teeth break through its voice, cutting it off with a wet gasp, warm and bubbling out where its throat had once been. The golden wolf tore her teeth away, the flesh of the creature's throat ripping away with them. The creature did not live long enough to know what form its final change would take, what it would become for its foolishness, but it was alive long enough to feel the wolves tear into its broken body, embracing it in the way that wolves have always embraced rabbits.

Time's Torn Seam
A. J. Van Belle

"You were a femme boy, Kendra. Now you're a femme. I fail to see the problem." Luciano spun in his office chair and swirled lazy fingers over the plexiglass window behind him. It looked out on the pale concrete buildings of the medical complex where we'd spent the last week while I tried to settle into my new body.

I didn't back away from his desk, but I wanted to. A sinkhole opened in my chest the day I woke up after the transplant, and the hole only grew worse every time I tried to talk Luciano into finding me an alternative. "*You* used to call me a femme boy to tease me for being skinny. That was never my gender identity. And the name," I said for the fiftieth time since the transplant surgery, "is Kendrick. Always was, always will be. I never signed any forms to change my name."

Luciano cackled. "You never signed any forms to change your body, either. Yet here we are."

No sense telling the guy that jokes about body transplants aren't funny. Especially not when the body being swapped out was bitten by a thousand Froyan tarantula-like slime molds with exoskeletons. When I thought I was doing a simple job gathering data on Froya's atmosphere but ended up with so little left of my muscle and bone, there was no chance of repair. No sense of the sacred with this guy. The machines could barely keep my old heart beating long enough to transport my carcass to this planet and all he wanted to do was listen to himself being clever.

I closed my eyes for a long moment. Bartered with myself: *if I can zip my lips now and stop trying, I'll go to the cafeteria and buy myself one of those drinks that has no name but it tastes like really good chocolate even though I know it's not made from—*

Shut up! Don't pawn me off with a treat, you petty bastard. If Luciano can't give me an answer, who will?

"There has to be some option," I said. "Put the request in the system. It doesn't have to be soon. I can wait. But let me do this before you drop me off on New Venus. I heard they don't have the tech there yet. It could be decades."

"My dear girl," Luciano began.

"Kendrick. My name is Kendrick. And I'm not a girl." I still couldn't get used to the sound of my new voice. It was a lovely alto. And listening to it felt like someone squeezing my neurons through the wringers of an on-planet hover-pod wash.

"My dear Kendrick-a," he went on, so smoothly I didn't know if he was even conscious of butchering it, "you are a fortunate, fortunate woman to have the body you do." He almost smirked. Or did I imagine that? "A very nice body indeed."

I put both palms on his desk and leaned forward. Not as intimidating a move as it would've been when I was twelve centimeters taller, but I could still invade his space. "Luciano, do not fucking tell me you're hitting on me."

He leaned back, twirling a stylus around his fingers. "My dear girl. You have a very nice body indeed because it has optimal liver and kidney function, a ratio of lean tissue to fat that is ideal for a female your age—the body's age, that is—and no significant health problems. You even have perfect vision." He tapped the stylus on his holo-projector. When turned off, it was nothing more than a small black box, but the implication was clear: the device contained every detail of information about me, in my former body as well as my new one. "Your previous body required corrective lenses. Wouldn't you count that change as a win?" I opened my mouth to speak, but he held a hand up. "And don't give me your bullshit about not being able to reach the top shelf in your closet. You may be shorter than you were in that old clunker of a body, but you're a woman of average height and you can use a step stool to reach the top shelf just like half the other women you know. What I'm saying, Kendra, is that you should be grateful."

"For a step stool?"

Luciano gave a disbelieving laugh. "For being alive." His tone said, *Are you stupid?*

I answered my own thought: *I don't know. Am I stupid?* Well, okay, that wasn't an answer. I *was* grateful to be alive. He was even right about a thing or two. This body was a new one grown in the specialized labs here on RU4, a planet devoted entirely to medical research facilities. The new body was the equivalent of twenty-four years old, a helluva jump back in time from the old body. Which was sixty-one. Not exactly a human antique by spacefaring standards, but it had some old injuries, muscles that twanged like a guitar string wound too tight, things like that. Bloody poop from time to time.

I took a deep breath. "Luciano. I know this is a good body. It's a great body, in fact. And you and your team saved my life. I *am* grateful for that. More than I know how to say. But . . . about this body. It's a great one for *someone else.* Someone who fits it. The problem—the problem is that it's not *my* body."

For the first time since I'd walked into the room, Luciano stopped fidgeting. He smiled sadly. "That's where you're mistaken. Kendrick. Kendra. Doesn't matter. You can call yourself whatever you want. The thing you're missing, the thing you're not adjusting to . . . is that this *is* your body. It's *yours,* kid. You get to keep it. For the rest of your life. It'll take a while to get used to it. It's that way for every single person who has a body transplant. The brain wakes up in a whole new shell and it doesn't know where the fingertips end or what shape the nose is, and when you look in the mirror you see someone else staring back at you. That's every transplanted brain ever, honey."

"Oh, for fuck's sake, Luce, we used to be colleagues. Equals. We're still equals. I've known you for five years and you never used to call me *honey.*"

"I should have started sooner. It has a ring to it. I like calling you honey."

I tossed my hands in the air in exasperation. "You're not half as funny as you think you are. Anyway, you know I've plead my case to the doctors. And I'll tell you, no one in the room was listening. Half of them were probably composing their grocery lists in their heads while I was talking, and the other half were taking a nap. But you? I thought you would at least be sympathetic. Maybe pull some strings for me. I'm not asking for a miracle. Just asking to come back here and have a second surgery when an XY-chromosome body is ripe."

Luciano shook his head and looked down at the stylus in his hands. "I've *been* listening, Kendrick." At least he cared enough to say my name right this time. "I do care. I just can't work miracles. I can't magically make the Council change the law for you." He sighed. "Look, we're not leaving RU4 until two days from now when they discharge you from post-transplant therapy," he said. "Why don't you go have some fun? Look around at the hothouses? Enjoy yourself."

So I did. Wandered down the hall into one of the big greenhouses, a high-ceilinged, warehouse-sized space where the RU4 doctors grew the bodies. The perfectly shaped, perfectly inanimate human forms steamed in their half-shell beds. Great palm fronds took up half the air space. You couldn't walk without brushing into them. Steam rose from vents in the floor, puffing around the bodies with their perfectly plump cheeks, flushed with health. Every color body, every shape and size. They grew fast compared to the homegrown old-fashioned way, but they were still a slow process. Not a single one in this room was ripe yet.

I received the only one they had that was ready. No others would be mature for months. But I could wait months. I *would,* if I had to. I would argue my case at the Interplanetary Council. Bug them so much I'd get them to change the law so a second transplant would be allowed if the first body didn't match the recipient's gender identity.

I looked around to make sure no attendants were nearby. When I was sure no one would see, I trailed my fingers over the edge of one of the half-shell coffin-cradles.

I don't know if you should do that, I said to myself. Same damn voice as the one asking for the chocolate-not-chocolate drink. *What if it's like a butterfly's wing or something? Maybe if you touch it, it won't grow anymore. Just like a butterfly can't fly if you rub the powder off its wing.*

That wouldn't make any sense, I told myself. I didn't want to admit I almost thought it *did* make sense though, in some way I couldn't name. Didn't matter, I was gonna touch the damn thing anyway.

The body was an XX, a little too "young" in greenhouse terms to be ready for a brain. Skin a peachy gold, chest rising and falling with steady breaths like someone asleep. So lifelike I was almost afraid to wake her.

The arm was warm and soft to my touch. The skin felt alive and tender. Like my daughter's skin when she was little, when I hugged her goodnight.

I pulled my hand back. This was not a person. Not yet. Just a receptacle waiting for a brain.

I hugged my arms across my waist, and my new body's own skin felt as *other* as the fresh-grown corpse in its shell.

Someone came to stand beside me. "A beautiful sight, isn't it?" The voice was smooth and low, and it belonged to a person in a white coat with a name tag that said *Dr. Acevedo.* She had golden skin, four yellow braids, and a severe brow line. I remembered her from the second row of doctors in the room where I gave my speech. When I begged them all to consider making a formal request to the Council on my behalf, Dr. Acevedo sat still and blank-faced.

She leaned closer to me. "The regulations are wrong."

The backdrop sound of steam vents gave us privacy. A few other people milled around the place, plant technicians adjusting the temperature, watering and trimming the plants. And medical technicians checking the bodies and adjusting their cradle-coffins' settings. But none in our corner of the greenhouse.

I kept my voice as low as hers. "What are you saying?"

"I'm saying all the doctors are having a bonfire at RU4's best beach tonight, and I plan to beg off sick. Because I have a patient who needs me."

"You mean me? You mean you want to—but there aren't any—" I looked around at the coffins, at the unripe bodies.

Her smile pitied my slowness. "Not here. And you're not the patient I mean. Come with me."

A few minutes later, we were in her office with the door closed. A tall, masc-presenting person stood in front of the window, arms crossed, tapping one foot. The person turned at the sound of the door. Thirty-ish, they had long, dark-brown hair in a ponytail and wore light makeup. They also had great musculature, the kind I envied but never had the discipline to achieve. Their brow wrinkled and their lips parted in an anxious expression.

"This is Ashley," Dr. Acevedo said. "She's a trans woman who came here to RU4 in the hopes of a transplant to a double-X chromosome body. Back on her home world, they told her the rules."

"But I thought if I came here and pleaded my case," Ashley said, "they would see it *is* medically necessary. I'm in the *wrong body.*"

Dr. Acevedo's sharp eyebrows quirked. "Just like you, Kendrick. She came all this way, and all they could do was tell her the rules again: that transplants to match the correct body to a patient's gender identity aren't considered medically necessary. I believe the rules are wrong. That's why I'm offering to risk my career to do the right thing by the two of you. But if we do this, it has to be tonight."

"You're proposing a swap." I looked at my smooth, pretty hands. No, not my hands. At least, maybe not for long. I looked at Ashley's hands, square and solid. Hairier than my originals had been, but who was I to complain? I'd still be getting a thirty-year jump on my old body. "When can we start?"

Dr. Acevedo held up her palm. "Wait a second. We need to make sure this is a good deal. For both of you." She turned to Ashley. "You'll be getting a fresh, lab-grown body. No known health problems, made to last you a good long time. But, apart from that, does it suit you? Can you be confident you'll be more at home in that body than the one you were born in?"

Ashley looked me up and down. "I don't have much of a choice, do I?" She smiled. "But it looks just fine to me. Uh—I mean—Kendrick, *you* look just fine." She bit her lip. "I'm sorry. This is a very unusual social situation. I'm not sure how to talk about your body—that's not really yours—that might soon be mine—oh, dear."

"It's fine," I said. A relaxed chuckle came out of me due to habit, but the fact was, I felt pretty giddy. So this was for real. I might be about to get back to a body that fit me. Tonight. Now, after I'd given up hope, it was really happening. "I'm not sure whose body is whose right now, to be honest."

Ashley gestured to her chest. "So. Uh. What do you think? Does this suit?"

"Well. I have to say. If I get your body as a transplant, for the first time in my life, I'll be a handsome devil. If I do say so myself."

Ashley laughed.

"I guess—the only thing is—any health problems I should know about? You know, does testicular cancer run in the family or something? Anything else I need to be on the lookout for?"

Ashley bit her lip again. "Not that I know of."

❖ ❖ ❖

We met at the operating room at midnight. Dr. Acevedo had Ashley stretch out on an operating table first and started her IV. She pulled a curtain across the middle of the room to divide us and had me take my place on an identical table. Once she put the IV in, the next thing I knew was—

—nameless space. I knew my own existence and felt the passage of time. But time was ripped away from physical dimension. Spacetime torn at its seam. I had no sense of anything tangible.

When I had my first transplant, this feeling-not feeling state scared me. This second time, I knew what to expect. I also knew where I was because they showed it to me after the first surgery, on a post-transplant tour of the lab. So I saw it with my brand-new, 20/20 eyes: a glass cylinder filled with blue-green gel the same density as a human brain, so the brain remains suspended. Soft and surrounded, protected from harm. Someone could shoulder-butt that cylinder and the brain wouldn't be jostled, not with all the gel cushioning it had.

No, the brain isn't in danger from outside forces. It's only in danger from an inside force, one that's part of everything. Time is the enemy of the brain in suspension. Without a body, even with the best gel suspension science has to offer, a brain can only last a few hours.

From the inside, when you're the gray matter in your secure little nest, you don't see anything.

You can hear, though. They found out early on that brains deteriorate if you leave 'em with no stimulation, even for an hour. People whose brains went through pure nothingness in the cells didn't do so well. They lost a lot of function and had to fight their way through months of rehab after their transplants.

So the docs hooked up some vibration sensors and figured out a way to transmit the sound waves through the gel in a way that would stimulate the auditory centers of the brain. And they took to playing music in the operating room to keep those brains entertained: interplanetary synth, New Space Age jazz, pop music from 300 years ago. Whatever works to give the neurons something to bop along to.

Then they found out it works even better if they talk to you. So the surgeons started narrating the whole process: *I'm connecting the trigeminal nerve now. You'll be able to feel your face! Isn't that splendid?* And: *I just noticed my shoelace is untied. Can't tend to it now! Too busy patching up the walls of this vertebral artery. We do want to make sure your brain has a good blood supply, don't we? And—there. Just like new. I was only worried for a second.*

Last time I was in the cell, they were playing Mozart. Now, Dr. Acevedo was playing something with an intricate lead guitar riff, a lot of heavy bass, and a vocalist who should have been in opera. I let the sound shape my whole awareness, because it was all I had. Once I settled into that, and it gave me some sense of shape, I tried to imagine reaching out to see if I could touch the walls of the cell. Couldn't make the imagining happen, though. Nothing to reach with. And there was no boundary, no space to move at all. I might as well have been in outer space, light years from a solid object.

Fear rose up in this gray liminal space. I didn't know how I knew fear, with no heart to race or armpits to sweat. But it was here with me nonetheless, in this endless nothingness.

I pushed it down. Grabbed onto the bass line, let it anchor me. *I'm still here. I'm still real. I'm still me.*

"Oh. Shit." Dr. Acevedo's voice had that understated quality that means a flaming asteroid is about to hit the planet and we'd better all get ready for the shockwave to flatten us. "Ashley? Are you awake yet?"

There was a dull groan in a voice that sounded all too familiar because, for one week, it had come from my own lips. Ashley, I gathered, was not awake.

"Shit. Shit. Shit." Dr. Acevedo's footsteps paced back and forth across the room.

C'mon, Doc, tell me what's wrong! I had no mouth to say the words.

Her rapid footsteps retreated to the other side of the room. The music stopped.

"Kendrick. I don't know if you can hear me."

Loud and clear, buddy! I had no lips. No tongue. No way to let her know I was still in here, awake and aware.

The fear returned. Empty, dead-cold, endless nothingness. A shaking hand or tremulous breath—that wasn't fear. I knew that now. Terror was isolation. From everyone. And everything. From even the body that made fear known.

"There's been a—a problem," Dr. Acevedo said. "The body. The body that *was* Ashley's. It's not—not viable anymore." The doctor's voice shook, but she managed to get the words out in a steady stream. "She was walking around with an aneurysm in her internal carotid artery. Likely no one knew about it since it hadn't ruptured. And it probably would have been okay for a while longer if it weren't for the surgery. But with the temporary severing of the artery, the pressure from the clamp was too much. It ruptured. Even with the support from our equipment, Ashley's former body bled out while I had my hands full with the lab-grown body. If I'd stopped mid-transplant, Ashley's brain would have died. Without question. And then we might have lost both of you. There's no other body for you, Kendrick." She let out a sob. "I'm sorry."

I wanted to take a deep breath and steady myself. But I had no lungs. I wanted to look away, toward the place where the corner of the room faded into shadow. Or walk away from Dr. Acevedo until I composed myself.

I could do nothing. I was a consciousness made of stardust, suspended in ether.

Maybe there was a way, a body on a neighboring planet that could be shipped here posthaste. I did the mental math—the only kind of math I could do, now—and found it wouldn't work. The nearest planet was sixteen hours away by the fastest ship, and a brain lasts no more than six hours in suspension.

"I'm sorry," Dr. Acevedo choked out again in a broken voice. "I should have left well enough alone. I'll turn in my medical license. There's no future for me after this."

Not your fault. The regulations are wrong. Not you. You tried.

A long, long pause followed. I drifted through spiral nebulae, flung aloft on solar winds.

After what seemed an age, her voice cut through the darkness again. "There's no future for you, either, Kendrick? Is there?" She must have been close to the glass indeed, because her words were a whisper but I heard them perfectly.

I drifted down from my dance with cosmic dust enough to wonder: Ashley's expression when I asked about problems. Was that just shyness I saw? Or shiftiness? Did her gaze slide sideways? I couldn't remember. Did she know she had a weak blood vessel in her skull? It didn't matter if she knew or not. The thing was done.

My sense of self faded into a twilight awareness. I existed and didn't. I was Kendrick and I was stardust.

In the space between matter and nothingness, I knew I would make this choice again. Better to risk the void than live in a body that wasn't me.

Still here. But mute.

Trapped.

With no body.

Spiraling away into nothingness, like sand blown by the wind.

Medusa Tattoo $450
Violet Mourningstarr

As long as my child never knows the humming buzz
Of apotropaic and ophidian metaphors
Little I care
That I hear the humming buzz of serpentine and
Powerlessness similes.
Through every needle pass I transform, transformed by
The searing pain.
What? The Evil Eye and sleeveen imagery?
How many needed to be hurt for this to trend.

—Medusa Tattoo $450
Imitation poem of "The Dying Lover" by Gustave Kahn

There Is No Subtlety, Only Rage
Stephanie Rabig

"The fuck are you doing here?"

Thomas Mitchell ("Mitch to my friends!" he was fond of saying. Everyone called him Thomas) stared at his prodigal "son," who was standing on the doorstep, clutching his phone like a lifeline. He'd heard the news, then. Thomas smirked.

"Come to congratulate me on the decision? I told you, sooner or later God wins."

"God had nothing to do with this shit."

"Watch your tone," he said. "I don't have to let you in." Probably should have changed the security gate code and told the guard that he was off the list of approved visitors.

This wasn't actually his son; it was his daughter, but he refused to give him the dignity of still using his original name, not until he'd apologized for the bad publicity he'd caused. He'd made the horrific announcement during his eighteenth birthday dinner of all times (that meal had cost over $2,000; the entire family had been there, and he'd pulled *that*) and then left home.

By all rights, he should've disowned him until he came to his senses and was ready to take his old life back. But, Thomas thought, he was a much kinder man than 'Spencer' (as he now called himself) and his degenerate friends liked to assume.

"I need to talk to you," Spencer said, hurrying inside, still death-gripping his phone.

"Need a loan? Get some girl in trouble at exactly the wrong time? Oh, wait—you can't. *Son.*"

Spencer's face turned red. "Nothing like that. I thought . . . I don't know what I thought," he said, suddenly looking as confused and lost as he used to back in high school when he'd lose a debate against him or his mother. "It's been seven years."

"And you thought I would've changed my entire belief system? Over what? You?"

"You honestly haven't rethought—"

"Why would I? I told you, didn't I, that someday you'd come crawling back? And here you are."

"I'm not crawling anywhere. You've seen the protests, the way people are reacting. I thought maybe, reading some of their stories, you'd . . . hell, it was too much to think you'd change your mind, but maybe you'd have some sympathy. People are going to die because of this."

"They're only going to die if they try something stupid," he huffed, heading for his liquor cabinet. "Drink?"

"No, thank you."

"Suit yourself. You were always too quick to fall for a sob story, kid. Some girl ends up taking an herbal concoction that a dumbass on TikTok recommends, she deserves what she gets."

"Okay, fine, we'll go with that example. Can you just imagine, for a minute, how absolutely desperate you'd have to be to take advice like that? How scared?"

"Should've kept her legs closed, then."

"Jesus Christ," Spencer muttered. "Where's mom?"

"Out on tour," he said. "And I'm sure she's celebrating tonight."

"I'm sure," Spencer echoed, looking disappointed.

How had they raised such a delusional child? Thomas wondered, not for the first time. Thinking he was a boy when he'd been born a girl; expecting his mother and father to change everything about their lives and beliefs just because he fell in with some liberal dipshits in high school. Now here he was, on what should be a fantastic night, staring at him like *he* was the disappointment.

"You still living with your little psychic friend?"

"Brenna is—"

"And she didn't 'see' this coming?" he grinned. Spencer didn't smile back, and he shrugged and took a drink.

His phone rang then, and he held up a finger at Spencer, telling him to wait a minute. He headed into the bedroom and took his phone from the charger. It was his wife, Phyllis, and he smiled as he headed back to the parlor.

"Hiiii, honey," she exclaimed, and he laughed. Phyllis did like her wine, and it didn't surprise him she was a little tipsy now. She and the other speakers on her pro-life tour had to be over the moon.

"Hi," he said. "Feeling good?"

"Feeling *amazing*," she replied. "You heard?"

"Of course I did! Congratulations, sweetheart."

"Couldn't have done it without all your hard work," she said, and he nodded in agreement. Though he hadn't won his latest bid for re-election, he'd accomplished a lot during his years in Congress.

"True," he said. "Guess who's here? 'Spencer'."

"Oh! Has she finally come to her senses? Ms. Barrett at church is always asking about her, and I keep saying that—"

"No, nothing like that. I think he's after an apology."

Spencer shook his head. "I know better."

"Then why are you here?" Thomas asked, putting Phyllis on speakerphone.

"This isn't something to celebrate," he said. "Can't you see that? Most Americans—"

"If most Americans like the idea of murdering babies, that's for them to eventually take up with God," Phyllis said (well, slurred). "Doesn't mean we have to stand by and let them. You should let this be a wake-up call for you, you know. Things always come back around to the proper way of . . . of doing things," she finished with a giggle. "Imma go. Just wanted to say I love you! And sweetie, I'll pray for you."

"Please, don't."

"Don't backtalk your mother," Thomas said, looking back to Spencer as he ended the call. "So, are you done whining? Is there anything else you wanted? If the answer's no . . . " He trailed off, nodding toward the door.

"I wish you and mom would *get it*!"

"Okay, that's enough. You feel like coming back, you can do that when you've got a better hold on your temper."

He ushered Spencer outside and locked the door, and then contacted the guard to make sure that Spencer actually left. Back when he'd been his daughter, before he'd been brainwashed, Spencer had loved to wander the grounds.

He could have that luxury again once he came to his senses.

Thomas took a deep breath and let it out on a sigh but had a little trouble drawing the next one.

He closed his eyes tightly and concentrated, succeeding in taking another deep breath only a few seconds later. But he couldn't shake the feeling that . . .

That what? Someone was watching him? No, that wasn't quite it. But something was *wrong*.

Where? There couldn't be someone else in the house, the alarms would have gone off. He had changed the code for those multiple times over the past seven years; Spencer couldn't have given those to any strangers.

He started hyperventilating, and nearly flinched out of his slippers when his phone rang.

Just the guard, it turned out, replying with the news that Spencer was gone.

"Are you all right, sir?" he asked, and Thomas cursed himself for allowing whatever worry had suddenly taken hold of him to show in his voice.

"Yes, yes, I'm fine."

"If Spencer comes back, do you want me to let him in?"

"No," he quickly answered. "I think we've said all we have to say to each other."

He thought momentarily about asking the guard to call for his physician, but instead hung up the phone. There was no reason for his heart beating too fast or it being difficult to breathe; those weren't symptoms of a heart attack.

Not a heart attack. A panic attack. Spencer's little friend, the girl who claimed to be psychic—they'd let Brenna into their home, fed her, and she'd repaid them by screaming at them to go away when he and Phyllis had gone to her apartment to retrieve Spencer after that disastrous eighteenth birthday dinner—she'd claimed to have them sometimes. There hadn't been anything attacking her, no reason to panic in her environment at all. Just attention-seeking.

This wasn't a panic attack, he tried to tell himself, even as some unnamed force in his brain took over, telling him the threat was *right there*, even if it couldn't tell him what that threat was. It was just seeing Spencer again. Being reminded of a time when he'd still had an ounce of hope that his child would come back.

But he wouldn't, he thought, as his heart rate finally began to slow again. He wouldn't, and that was for the best. No matter how moral the parents were, some kids were just bad eggs.

He finished his drink, put the glass in the sink for his maid to take care of, and went to bed.

Less than an hour later, he awoke in a pool of sweat, wanting to scream and having no idea as to why.

❖ ❖ ❖

"I think I might come home early."

"What?" Thomas asked. Phyllis made it a point of pride to always finish out her speaking engagements—even that time she'd tested positive for COVID, she hadn't felt poorly enough to even think about letting her audience down.

"I just don't feel well. Last night was supposed to be perfect, and instead it was awful. I felt like I couldn't breathe."

He'd been about to dismiss her with a comment about not drinking as much tonight, but at those words he paused. "Really?"

"I knocked on Amy's door—she used to be a nurse, remember—and she said it was a panic attack, of all things. I've never had one of those; I'm stronger than that."

"I know you are," he soothed, deciding not to mention his own. He and Phyllis had been fighting against Roe v. Wade for decades; maybe last night had been a delayed reaction to all that tension suddenly gone.

That had to be it.

He realized then that his wife had said something else. ". . . what?" he asked.

"I said, I'll see you tonight."

"If you're sure," he said. "Love you."

"Love you, too."

He hung up and went to make breakfast, cracking three eggs into a bowl before setting a small pan on the front right burner and turning the heat on. He mixed some cheese and a tiny sprinkle of salt into the eggs and then poured it into the pan.

This was his usual breakfast, his comfort food; he'd had it almost every morning for the past five years.

Now, the minute the smell hit his nose, he felt an uncontrollable urge to vomit.

It came on so strong and so suddenly he didn't have time to lecture himself about the nonsense of it. He barely made it to the bathroom and didn't quite make it to the toilet; he just doubled over and threw up in front of the sink. The vomit splattered on the floor, some of it hitting his slipper-clad feet and his bare ankles.

Shuddering, he rinsed out his mouth and shakily grabbed a hand towel to wipe off his skin. The slippers went straight into the trash—he'd buy a new pair. He hurriedly left the bathroom and shut the door behind him. He'd use the bathroom on the second floor until the maid had had a chance to take care of this one.

The sound of the smoke alarm made him curse. He'd left the stove on.

He ran to the kitchen and took the smoking pan off the burner. The smell of scorched eggs made his stomach roil again, but this time he was able to hold it down.

After a breakfast of dry cereal instead, he fielded a few calls from reporters looking for his reaction to the overturning of the legislation he'd built his political career fighting against. In the middle of the last call, fatigue suddenly hit . . . not the type he was used to, after a long walk or a busy day entertaining guests. Even thinking of the success of his life's goal couldn't break through the gray cloud suddenly enveloping him.

"Mr. Mitchell?" the reporter asked. "Are you all right?"

He realized then that he'd trailed off in the middle of a quote and forced himself to laugh. "Of course, of course! Just recovering from last night's celebration! I'm no spring chicken anymore."

The reporter chuckled. "Neither am I. Thanks for taking the time to talk to me, and congratulations again."

"To you, too." The reporter was one he'd become familiar with over his years as a Congressman, and it was nice to see the young man's support and friendliness hadn't gone away since his retirement.

Some people, he thought, Spencer's face appearing unbidden in his mind, knew the meaning of loyalty.

But the thought didn't hold the full measure of bitterness it should have. The gray was still there, pressing down, and all he wanted to do was go to sleep.

That might actually be a good idea, he thought. Everything would be normal again after a nap.

❖ ❖ ❖

Thomas awoke to the sound of his wife sobbing.

He scrambled out of bed, nearly tripping on the bedside rug, and hurried to the front door. Phyllis was curled up on the floor, crying her heart out.

"Phyllis!" he exclaimed, crouching down in front of her. Had she been mugged? Or had protesters gotten hold of her? He'd kill every last one of the selfish little pricks. "What happened? What's wrong?"

"I don't know!" she cried.

He rocked back on his heels, frowning. "What do you mean, you don't know?"

"I mean I've felt like this all day! Like this, or even worse. I haven't been able to eat anything; I couldn't even sleep on the plane."

"It's all right," he said, even as he tried to put everything together. He hadn't felt right since Spencer had come to visit . . .

When he'd gone to answer the phone, had he taken his drink with him or left it behind? He couldn't remember. Even if Spencer had put something in it as revenge, that didn't explain Phyllis's condition.

Still, the idea that this had something to do with Spencer wouldn't leave his mind.

"Come on," he said, helping his wife to her feet. "Let's get you to bed. I'll get you a nightcap."

At that, she managed a smile. "It's two in the afternoon."

"Then I'll get you an afternooncap." The joke was weak, but she smiled again, and he felt reassured as he led her to their room.

He helped her into bed, and then fetched her a drink before turning on Fox News for her, making sure the volume was low enough not to interfere with her nap. "There," he said. "You want me to lie down with you?"

"Yes, please."

He obliged, nearly falling asleep again before Phyllis suddenly doubled over, spilling her half-finished drink all over the sheets.

The drink. What if Spencer hadn't put something into his glass, but into the entire bottle?

He wrapped an arm around his wife's shoulders, asking her what was wrong, what was happening, what could he do.

In answer, she just let out a shriek of pain, and then patted at the wet sheets covering her legs. "There's too much, there's too much blood, I can't—"

"It's not blood!" he told her, nearly shouting in his panic. "You spilled your drink!"

She shook her head wildly. "I'm bleeding!"

"Phyllis, you are not hurt. Look at me. You're okay."

She didn't listen, didn't look at him, just kept patting at her legs over and over again. Just as he was about to get out of bed and call the doctor, she let out a final cry and flopped back, her eyes open and staring and still somehow terrified.

"Phyllis?" he whispered.

She didn't answer him, didn't move.

His hand was trembling as he checked for a pulse at her wrist, at her neck.

Nothing.

"Spencer," he whispered, slowly getting out of bed. Unable to look back at his wife, he stumbled out to the foyer and grabbed his car keys from the hook. Normally, he would call his chauffeur, but he wanted no witnesses to this drive.

❖ ❖ ❖

The minute Spencer opened the door to his apartment, Thomas barreled inside, his hands going for his child's neck. Spencer instinctively knocked him away—the self-defense lessons he'd paid for all those years ago had paid off, he thought wildly—and backed further into the apartment.

"What did you do?" Thomas shouted. "What the hell did you do?"

"What are you talking about?"

Brenna, drawn by the sound of his yelling, hurried into the living room. Thomas turned on her. "You! Were you in on this, too?"

"In on what?" Spencer asked, but there was something in his voice, and some knowledge in Brenna's eyes . . .

Play it close, Thomas thought, some semblance of his old cunning finally breaking through his anger and heartache. Don't let them know the extent of it yet.

"I haven't felt right since your visit. I've had panic attacks. Your mother has, too. I was sick at breakfast, and your poor mother woke up thinking she was lying in a pool of blood."

"Holy shit," Spencer whispered, even as Brenna smiled.

"It worked," Brenna said, that awful smile growing wider. She wouldn't be smiling on the stand, he thought. He'd see her put away for the rest of her miserable life for this, and that was only if the jury didn't give her the death penalty.

"What worked?" he asked, struggling to keep his voice calm.

"People can only *feel* so much before something breaks," Brenna said. "That break can create a hell of a lot of power. Spencer and I used it. To show you what people have gone through."

"None of that shit," he snapped. No jury would believe in curses, he thought, even as he remembered Spencer's words: *I wish you and mom would get it.* "You put something in our drinks, didn't you? They'll be able to tell. I'll take that bottle straight to the police."

"I didn't do anything to your goddamn booze."

"Bullshit!" Thomas yelled. "You—" He cut off, clutching at his stomach as something there seemed to *pulse*, tightening to an unimaginable degree before finally letting him breathe again.

Relief only lasted for a few seconds before the pain was back, and he groaned and stumbled to a chair, sinking down into it. Brenna drew closer, taking his hand despite his best efforts to pull away.

"Yeah, those are contractions," Brenna said, before moving back again. "Specifically, what a little girl named Lilah felt over a decade ago. She died in childbirth. Baby didn't make it, either. Not surprising. She was only eleven years old."

Trying to ignore her words, the unsettling quiet fury in her voice, Thomas closed his eyes. She wasn't delusional, wasn't trying to make herself seem more interesting for attention, as he'd assumed for years. She was a goddamn witch.

"Take this back," he ordered. "Right now. I . . . I learned my lesson, all right?" If he could just convince them that this horrific experiment had worked, then he could get out of here, go to the cops—

No, not the cops. There was no way they'd believe him. But he knew other people, people who'd be more than happy to take care of the witch and his traitorous son.

"Now," he said. "Your mother and I will forgive you, if you take it back now."

Brenna looked to Spencer and smiled, then crouched down to his eye level and took both his hands in hers.

"No."

"*What*?" he shouted, before another contraction hit. "You . . . you listen to me! You have to stop!"

"No," she said again, and the fury he felt at her daring to deny him drove bone-deep. "I want you to feel it. I want you to know. Not in theory, but *know*. I want you to feel every goddamn scrap of pain that you and your smug, controlling friends have ever caused the rest of us."

"Spencer," he panted. "Your mother's dead. You going to let this bitch kill me, too?"

"There a reason your life should matter more than all those you spent years trying to sentence to death?"

"You . . . you . . ." he gasped, and then Brenna let go of one of his hands, motioning to Spencer to take it.

"I want to try something," Brenna said. "And I need you to watch over me."

❖ ❖ ❖

As his father pressed back further in the chair, ashen-faced, Spencer closed his eyes. He'd had out-of-body experiences several times, and for most of those he'd been keeping an eye on Brenna as she ventured further than he dared, providing a tether to the waking world, giving her a voice to focus on and come back to should she start to fade away.

She'd spoken to spirits before in this shadowy aspect of their world, but never so *many*.

There were hundreds—thousands—and he felt his heart break when he realized how young some of them were.

Brenna floated among the spirits, clasping a hand here, giving a shoulder a gentle touch there. As she did, he saw their stories right along with her.

Mara. Ectopic pregnancy. A Catholic hospital that wouldn't perform the surgery, not enough time to get elsewhere, almost half of her body's blood gone when her fallopian tube burst.

Selene. Mother of two children, discovered her third pregnancy soon after her husband had been laid off and two days after Dr. George Tiller had been murdered. Terrified of going to a clinic for an abortion, she'd had the baby. And she and her husband had tried, tried so hard, but all three of their children had been taken away when a welfare check had found they 'couldn't provide'. She'd killed herself.

Amirah. Newly twenty-one, loved partying with her friends. Her periods had always been irregular, and she hadn't realized she was pregnant until she was too far along for her state's regulations. The baby had been poisoned by the alcohol in her system and hadn't lived through the birth. She'd thrown herself back into her old life, but out of desperation and grief rather than fun now, and she'd died in a car crash six months later.

Olivia. Pregnant at fifteen, her mother promised her that she would drive her to get an abortion. Instead, she'd driven her to her aunt's isolated home, where she'd stayed until she had the baby. There were complications. Neither survived the birth.

Harper. Visited by her father every night, she'd known it was only a matter of time. When she'd lost even the hope of being able to get an abortion when the inevitable happened, it had been the last trauma her young mind could cope with, and she'd hung herself.

Elena. Pregnant after her abusive husband tampered with her birth control, she searched online for abortifacients. She'd been careful, but herbal remedies are fiddly, and she'd taken too much.

Maeve. Beaten to death by her uncle when he'd discovered she was planning to 'kill his baby.'

Though he didn't feel it, not like his father did, the knowledge flooded Spencer's mind, all the stories and pain and panic and fear. And he wasn't even making physical contact with the spirits, not like Brenna.

He started to call her back, and then he saw a spirit he'd spoken with several times before. His great-uncle, who had been trans just like him. Only this time, as Brenna took his hands in hers, Spencer saw.

He knew his uncle had died young—just looking at his spirit had told him that much—but he hadn't been able to find much in the family records, and after one drunken rant about how 'sick' he'd been, his mother had remained closemouthed.

A family refusing to accept who he was. Institutionalization. Raped by the guards to 'fix' him and died when the baby died inside of him, and he hadn't been given medical care.

He met his uncle's eyes, wishing more than anything he could rush over and hug him, but today he had to maintain Brenna's contact to the outside world. He mouthed "I'm so sorry," and his uncle gave him a sad smile in return.

The names went on and on and on, the stories, so many people dead because a theoretical baby had mattered more than their actual lives, and finally he screamed Brenna's name.

"It's too much!" he called to her, hoping she could still hear him. She was surrounded by spirits now. "We have to go!"

"I have to hear them," she called back, her voice hoarse with tears. "They deserve to be heard, Spencer!"

"They do! And we'll hear them! But not all at once. We can't. Remember our plan, Bren. Spread it out."

She didn't answer, and for a few seconds he feared the worst. Then, the light that had surrounded her since the moment she'd stepped into this realm flared out sun-bright, and when Spencer opened his eyes again, they were on the floor of the apartment.

Brenna wiped tears away and crawled over to him, and he hugged her tightly. "You okay?"

"I will be."

"Did it work?"

It would be based on joy, Brenna had told him, when they'd stayed up half the night ranting and coming up with the idea. As much as people they knew online liked to snark about how "if men could give birth abortion would be free everywhere," Spencer knew better than most that some men could indeed give birth, and some women were perfectly cozy with the idea of "choice for me but not for thee." Gender wasn't the deciding factor; cruelty was. Anyone who heard of the Supreme Court decision, Brenna had finally said, and been happy about it.

"I think so," Brenna whispered. "When we left . . . when we left, everyone was smiling."

Across the country, forced-birthers began to scream.

Come Here, Ofelia
Cynthia Gómez

They found her at the start of the first spring rains. The
culverts were clogged with leaves and surgical masks and used
needles that surely must have swirled around her for days,
and when the officers clambered down the banks to find her
they came away with rotting leaves thick and slimy on their
clothes. She had carried with her a collection of weights and
barbells, the modern version of a Mary Wollstonecraft, and
she had placed them in a backpack that she then strapped
onto her chest. Suicide without the bomber, one of the
detectives thought to herself, the only woman in the group,
and then felt a flash of shame.

As they pulled her from the water, careful as they were,
her pants snagged and pulled down on a branch, and they
could see the beginning swell of her belly, a slight curve that
answered many questions and spawned a thicket of others.
After days in the water, any trauma that might have been
written on the body would be harder to find, and the detectives
huddled over her swollen frame had no way to satisfy their
desire to know if she'd been assaulted, the question that rolls

itself off the tongue of nearly every homicide detective when a girl's body is found in a place it doesn't belong.

A Missing Persons file sprawled over the lead detective's desk began to plug in the gaps, even as the coroners were scraping underneath every fingernail and running over her scalp a comb of the kind usually reserved for nits. She'd been a straight-A student, a full scholarship to Stanford firmly in hand, with plans to study English and head abroad to Oxford or Cambridge her junior year. The note, of sorts, she'd left, was her copy of Hamlet, splayed out on her desk against a dark red Stanford sweatshirt and open to Act Three, Scene One, underlined three times in a bright neon green: *My honored lord, you know right well you did.*

Who the honored lord might be was easy to determine after a few minutes with her surrendered phone, but her missing hours were bracketed neatly inside his alibi: he'd been two hours away visiting his fiancée and her family, his cell phone locating data firmly in place, and his crumpled face when he learned of the fetus, thirteen or fourteen weeks at the most, told them what they needed to know. The reaction of her parents to the same news was as if a rapacious god had pulled open the front of their house, and they were blinking at the light and the dust.

Two floors down from Homicide and Missing Persons were the county courthouses themselves, and behind one judge's chambers a set of files that might have told more of her story, if the detectives had felt the need to keep combing, if her loaded backpack hadn't told the tale so simply and well, if there'd been any sign of a struggle or if the boyfriend's (ex-boyfriend's) alibi hadn't held. Notes from a judicial bypass hearing, eight days prior to the day she told her parents she was going to work and instead left the book's spine broken on her desk.

The notes captured nothing of the girl herself, confidence stripped away from her in the chilly room, as if it had never grown out of her at all but had merely been a coat that snagged on a hook as she passed through the doors; of her voice that insisted on wavering as she tried to explain that no, telling her parents that she was getting an abortion would be the end of everything, and in that moment all the polished words and phrases she'd used to line her life just fell away from her, blown out like a candle. Ofelia had no way to tell the judge just how and why every door in her life would slam shut, how her parents would turn her into Rapunzel, into Rafaela from The House on Mango Street, a book she'd dismissed as overwrought and overprescribed to girls like her. But every metaphor abandoned her, shrinking in the corner, silent.

The judge's eyes slid over the girl, neat as a pin, a single silver cross around her throat, one brown eye and one hazel, a strawberry-colored birthmark at the edge of her chin. "Did your parents give you that cross?"

"Yes, Your Honor, for my sixteenth birthday." They'd enclosed it in a white Bible, their eyes full of tears at this milestone of their eldest daughter, as if imagining the day when she'd zip shut the last of her suitcases and walk out of their lives.

"That doesn't sound like a set of parents who don't care about their child."

Ofelia knew this kind of silence, the kind that expected to be filled.

"Yes, Your Honor."

"How about you talk to them? If they still say no, you come back in a week or so and we'll talk again." And the judge made a set of marks on the file in front of her, the movements so slight and few that Ofelia imagined there must be a code, an acronym, that existed or had evolved for girls like her, enough to capture her story for the staff who would close her file and set it neatly back on its shelf.

Ofelia's boyfriend had no idea of the hearing with the judge, or of the reason for it, and even if he had that wouldn't have helped him understand what he began seeing the day after the detectives came. It started off with little things he could dismiss or reason away: the muddy footprints on their crumbling balcony made no sense, of course, but when he looked more closely he could imagine they weren't in the shape of feet at all, simply a wavering outline that only the paranoid could imagine as such, and he called his fiancée to scrub them off.

But that night he dreamed that Ofelia was straddling him, her thick soccer thighs that he'd loved, riding him in a way she'd discovered thrilled her, and her belly was flat and smooth, her voice strong and clear, but she was shouting again and again: *you know right well you did.* When he woke up the bed was soaked, pooling over his chest and running down onto the floor, clogged with leaves thick and slimy, and he knew without thinking just where the wetness was coming from, but what could he do, exactly? Who would he tell?

He lumbered to where his fiancée lay sleeping in their baby's room, her long fingers draped between the bars of the crib. He'd kill anyone who touched either of them, he'd always said. Of course, what to do if that someone was already dead?

The judge might have expected something if she'd imagined it were possible. She'd been harassed plenty of times, had bullets sent to her in the mail, had text messages from anonymous numbers calling her a *viscous cunt.* But she was unprepared for waking up one morning to a bedroom streaked with slimy leaves and mud flecked with hypodermic needles, muddy handprints on her daughter's bronzed baby shoes. She had seen a headline about a drowned girl found in a creek with weights strapped to her chest, but never connected it to anything. She'd never thought of Ofelia except to wonder once in passing about that meek young girl with the birthmark, if she had ever spoken to her parents and if they had risen to the occasion and put away their judgments to welcome a new life into the world.

The judge could never remember when it started after that. Whether what came first was the nausea thick on her tongue, as if there were a layer between herself and everything she might eat, like a strip of cheesecloth filtering out everything but bile, and the only things she could keep down were a strawberry smoothie and a ridiculously salty Coppa, sliced thin like flayed flesh; or if it was struggling to pull herself out of bed and feeling as though she was swimming up through layers of water. Thick with leaves. The question rattled inside as she knelt over the toilet, trying to count when her period had come last, this visitor she could have just as well done without now that she was nearly forty-three, this unwanted knocking every single month but to nothing, like kids ringing the bell only to flee down the hall.

There was no explanation for the printout that sat in her lap a week after Easter, lining up below reports of thyroid function and blood sugar, everything normal but this: *PPCT, positive, estimated gestational age 7-8 weeks per hCG levels*. It never occurred to her that it was anything other than a mistake. It had been more than a year since she'd been with a man, and in the ten minutes while the doctors huddled down the hall she scrolled through her phone, searching for articles on "false positive pregnancy tests," telling herself she knew better than to stumble into internet black holes.

Even as the cold gel slid over the ultrasound wand, the judge insisted to the technologist that there was no way this could be true: that like she'd told the advice nurse, her doctor, even the receptionist who made the appointment, it just wasn't possible, and then the ultrasound crawled across the screen in front of them both, watery and black and white and unmistakable, telling the same story as the tests run on urine and blood. The face of the tech shifted to an expression she must be used to wearing, one the judge herself had worn in her own way: for the teenagers who insisted as they held their mother's hands that the tests must be wrong, to please run them again, because there was no way that result could be right. It slid so easily into that mode, a practiced thing, a worn groove. *Are we still going with the "impossible" story?* this face seemed to say. *Seems to be a lot of immaculate conceptions around here these days.*

She flashed again to the night of the leaves, but the alarm systems from that night had shown nothing, every window lock and door undisturbed, and the ultrasound in front of her was making a lie of the camera feed. She was going to be one of those women, the second she opened her mouth. The messy ones, the ones who stuck to their stories even when the tests, the eyewitnesses, the photos in front of them were perfectly clear, and yet she could remember so many stupid women—not only women, mind—who insisted until the end, until the bailiff led them away, that the photos, the tests, the witnesses, were wrong. She'd never understood why they'd bother to tell such an obvious lie. Such a waste of time. There were no words she could imagine that wouldn't put herself in their company, that would erase the look from the technologist's face. She could feel herself shrinking inside her gown, and she meekly accepted the printouts they gave her and the appointments they made, the directions to the pharmacy to pick up prenatal vitamins and Diclectin for the queasiness.

With every day that her waistline expanded, she could feel herself shrinking in kind. Every morning she would lie very still, as if her old reality was waiting for her, like a jacket she'd left draped over a chair, and she could imagine it for a breath or two, perhaps three at the most, until the rush to vomit crumpled her onto the floor. The pink kidney-shaped basin, no matter how often she scrubbed it, always smelled rancid and sour, reminding her that this was still real, this story she seemed to have walked into without knowing the beginning or the end. Sleep was harder to reach every night, the slightest disturbance pulling her awake, and when she did dream she was always drowning. The worst dream was of herself, in the lake behind her childhood home, feet tangled in brown leaves rotting to slime, grasping at what felt like an outcropping of rock, only to feel it begin pushing her down, her arms and legs fighting the weight.

She remembered reading how a malnourished body when pregnant would cannibalize itself, and as she grew thinner she wondered if the baby was forcing her to do just that. One week she could tolerate nothing but kidney beans with pickled onions; the next, only a jar of sour cherries she stole from a neighbor's grocery delivery, a thing she'd never done in her life. She stood in the building's hallway swallowing half the jar of the incredibly sour fruit before she could stop herself. She imagined herself as anyone else would see her: skin the color of old milk and studded with bruises, eyes ringed with bumpy flesh in maroon giving over to purple, bright cherry flecks clinging to her hair. As she stumbled through her door still clutching the jar, she saw the words scrawled in her favorite lipstick on the surface of the fridge: *It killed Charlotte Brontë, you know.*

"Hyperemesis gravidarum," the doctor pronounced at her next visit. She had no intention of telling him she already knew the term, or just how she'd been led to it the night before. She could imagine a new rickety Latin phrase making its way into her chart: *pre-partum psychosis*. A door into a world of soft and bland things she could never use to hurt herself, the anxious fluttering around her belly, the rising mound they were protecting against her. Ha. And just who would protect her from it? She blanched at the word in her own brain, the *it*. Behind the doctor she could see the line graph of her weight, a dizzying descent into zones colored orange and then red.

"In most cases, it's already resolved itself long before this stage. If it hasn't, we don't have a lot of hope that it will improve. The impact I'm seeing in these tests is worse than I can ever recall. And we can expect it to get worse." She tried to imagine what she looked like through the notes on the screen: the ravages to organs and bones as the thing inside consumed her from within. His fingers grazed the screen and she recoiled, as though they had somehow touched her.

"What are you saying to me?"

"I'm saying you're only eighteen weeks. Termination is still an option." She could feel a fluttering inside her belly, just inside her rib cage, and she imagined a trapped creature beating its wing against the bars.

"I've never done anything like that." She hated her voice for its wavering. "I've never walked away from a challenge. Especially when it's not the baby's fault." It was what she held to when desperate young women flocked to her courtroom, this rush to protect them from a decision she knew they would surely regret. A thread of blood dripped onto the floor, her third nosebleed that morning.

"I understand." He held himself very still, the kind of silence that could sit as long as it needed to, until there was something to say. The fluttering grew stronger as she let her eyes close to imagine it, the lie she could create with the same skill she'd used to weave the story of the younger man who impregnated her and then disappeared. She could almost smell the chicken soup her neighbors would bring, see the cards slipping through the mail slot, consoling her on the terrible miscarriage that had come after all this time. Sleep returning, her organs slowly knitting their way back. When she spoke her voice was faint and thin, and she had to swallow twice and try again.

"Maybe—"

That was when the flutter became a thud, and she was throwing out her hands before she even understood that she was hurtling towards the floor.

❖ ❖ ❖

The judge called her daughter at college that night, dialing awkwardly around the cast on her right hand, plaster cradling the weakened bone that had cracked right down the middle.

"It wasn't like I was falling, so much as . . . like something was pushing me." *From inside,* she didn't let herself say, and she wondered just who her silence was protecting. Or what. The judge could hear her daughter suck in a deep breath.

"Mom, I'm so worried about you. Every time I talk to you it's like you've lost something else. Are you sure this is what you want?"

All those girls in her courtroom, so sure of what they wanted. She had asked just the same question of them. She felt the roiling in her stomach again, though she had eaten nothing all day.

"I'll call you back."

As she stood up from the toilet and wiped her mouth, she could feel the tug of the phone in her pocket, a line that could take her back to where no sex meant no babies; where she could walk more than a block without her body threatening to collapse, a sac of blood and bone wrapped around the growth inside her. She began to pace even though every step sent pain stabbing up her spine. She opened a browser on her phone and stared for minute after minute at the number before she hit "send."

"Thank you for calling Planned Parenthood. If this is an emergency—"

She never got to hear the rest.

The judge's daughter arrived on a red-eye from Chicago, just in time to see her mother being wheeled into surgery for the broken hip she'd sustained in a sudden fall in her bathroom. "Don't worry; the baby's going to be fine," they reassured the young woman as the gurney parted the surgery doors.

"And my mother? Is she going to be fine?" she shouted back before the doors swung shut.

The judge was placed on full bed rest, and her daughter canceled an internship in D.C. and put her fall semester on hold so she could care for her mother, hiring someone to dismantle the couch and coffee table in favor of a hospital bed. She winced the first time the patient was installed inside the monstrous thing and the home health aide pulled up and secured the locking sides. "Isn't that a little . . . extreme?" she asked the aide. "And if she falls again?" came the response, a little more clipped than it needed to be.

The judge seemed to her daughter to have emerged from surgery an even smaller version of herself, the locked bed rails a sort of reverse cocoon. The judge let reality TV babble all day long, when before she'd sneered at the producers' cheap manipulation of their stars, the predictability of every show. She submitted without protest to the locking bed rails and the daily blood draws, and she spent her hours somewhere neither dreaming nor waking, the space between them thin as a membrane.

The week after she arrived, the young woman sat down beside her mother's hospital bed, afternoon light weakening through the pink curtains, her hands clutching stacks of test results, spotted everywhere in red ink, and she took in a breath to ask again the question that had been beating inside her for days. But the judge must have read the question on her face, because before the young woman could say a word her mother's hands shot out into the air and her thin voice began babbling, like an incantation: "No, no, no, no, no, don't say it. Please. I won't do it. I promise. I promise."

The condo sank into summer and fall to the rhythms of the blood pressure monitor, the alarms for turning the patient's body against bedsores. By September, after two trips to the emergency room, it included twice-weekly visits of a dialysis machine. And always, any time of day or night, the retching into the basin, its shape a cruel reminder of the organs that had apparently given up the fight.

In the dark days after what should have been Thanksgiving, her mother's due date still five days away, the judge's daughter woke at 3 a.m. to find the bed rails down and the bathroom door locked against her, retching and sobbing sounds carrying through the wood.

"I said that, didn't I? I'm sorry. I remember you now. Oh no, oh no, I remember."

"Remember what, Mom? Please let me in!"

"I did this. I did this. You've been killing me for months, haven't you? Please don't kill me. Don't kill me anymore." The voice was low, thick, struggling.

"Mom? Who's there?" The door rattled in its frame and swung open, and the young woman clapped a hand over her mouth and ran scrambling for her phone.

At the hospital, as she gripped her mother's hands during every contraction, she told herself that there was no way she could have seen everything in that bathroom that her eyes insisted was there. The maroon puddle on the floor with a ring of baby teeth, in a room with no baby in it. That bloody mouth in her mother's face, opening wide and spitting onto the tiles a long yellow sash, or at least it must have been yellow once, *National Honor Society* in white lettering stained with red. The bathroom mirror, swinging open above their heads, scratched with tiny lettering neater than her mother's had ever been: *Come back in a week or so and we'll talk again.*

The baby came after twenty hours of labor, three pints of blood, and an emergency C-section that ended just before dawn. The judge's daughter, stiff and bleary in the visitor's chair, watched the nurse place the newborn girl on her mother's chest while another reached out with a washcloth to wipe the judge's matted hair from her face, sallow with what the doctors were warning could mean liver failure.

A little fist stabbed into the empty air, aiming for its mother's face. The nurse reached out to cover the tiny nails with a pair of peach-colored mitts, and the fist swung its way at her chin. The nurse's nervous laughter sounded forced. "What, you don't want to wear your mitts?" But then she caught the baby's gaze and the peach wool dropped to the floor.

The judge's voice sounded like it had been beaten within an inch of its life. It barely rose over the thrumming of the dialysis machine, the monitor ready to shriek when her blood pressure again shot dangerously low.

"Come here, Ofelia. Don't hurt Mama now."

"Ofelia? That's an unusual name." The nurse's eyes rested anywhere but on the baby's face, one brown eye and one hazel, the birthmark at the edge of the little chin.

"Oh, yes. That's her name." The judge's voice kept on fading. "And she's going to be a world-beater, aren't you? That's right. You're just going to set the world on fire."

The Graveyard
Ravven White

When I was a child,
darkness descended
upon my hallowed ground
as he laid his hands upon me
ripping screams from my lungs
undeveloped
unheard
undeserved
voiding my safety
and transforming my body
into a tomb of traumas
which he filled day by day

my body was not my own

When I was a young woman
freshly emerging into society,
emptying my premature graveyard

bone by bone
dust by dust,
a different man put his hands on me
seeking sanctino
for the brusies he bequeathed me
citing that his adornments were gifts
for my afterlife
my original traumas
engraved on broken headstones
markers that, he said
no one else would want to own
but that he would attempt to redeem

my body was not my own

When I was a weary woman
stricken by disease
spreading from my open graves
like thorny vines that only bloomed in blood,
a doctor laid his hands upon me
denying my pain, my vulnerability
and turned me away to die
in the shadows of my sepulcher
because my husband deserved children
my worth determined
by a desecrated tomb

The Graveyard

I required permission to exist
because my consicousness was not enough

my body was not my own

I am a forgotten woman
healing traumas I didn't deserve
afraid of hands that
are not my own
the shadow of men before me
shading my cemetary.
I wake at ungodly hours
haunted by dreams of
sapphire bruising and
terrified screaming
and even now,
after all these years,

my body is not my own

Trigger Warnings

A note about trigger warnings:

Trigger warnings are the informed consent of media. As strong believers in making horror fiction accessible to every individual reader, we have compiled a list of possible triggers found in the stories within *Mine: An Anthology of Body Autonomy Horror*. This list may not be exhaustive, so reader discretion is advised. If you feel trigger warnings spoil the genre, that's fair. Please stop reading from this point.

ALL FALL DOWN
> Assault, misogyny

BLEEDING AT HER ROOTS
> Child abuse (underage marriage mentioned), pregnancy, birth, violence, religion, lack of consent, misogyny

CHILD BRIDE
> Forced marriage, death

Come Here, Ofelia
Abortion, blood/gore, graphic medical situations, labor/birth, loss of bodily autonomy, suicide

D.E.B.
Ableism, body dysphoria, discussion of non-consensual surgery (off-page), lack of consent, physical assault, death (implied), violence, and discussion of global violence.

Feed Us
Abortion, blood/gore, body dysphoria, death of loved one, eating disorder, gendered language, graphic medical situations, labor/birth, loss of body autonomy, misogyny, pregnancy, violence

I Am a Weapon
Pregnancy, miscarriage, stillbirth, labor, use of the gendered term 'mother'

The Luthier's Muse
Unwanted affection, gore, relationship violence

Medusa Tattoo $450
Sexual assault theme

PRE-BABY BODIES
Postpartum depression, suicidal ideation

THE GRAVEYARD
Child abuse, lack of consent, loss of body autonomy, rape, sexual assault, violence

THE MAGICIAN ON HIS DEATHBED
Murder, loss of bodily control, institutionalization

THE RABBITS THAT MAKE US WOLVES
Animal death, gore, body dysmorphia/dysphoria

THERE IS NO SUBTLETY, ONLY RAGE
Abortion, blood/gore, child abuse (sexual, off-page), graphic medical situations, incest, intimate partner violence, labor/birth, lack of consent, loss of body autonomy, miscarriage, misogyny, pregnancy, rape, stillbirth, substance misuse, suicide, transphobia, violence

TIME'S TORN SEAM
Ableism, body dysphoria, gendered language, graphic medical situations, misogyny, transphobia

WOMB
Blood/gore, self-harm

The Authors

Brocklehurst, Kelly

Kelly Brocklehurst (she/her) is a queer horror writer, editor, and poet. She is the author of *Price Manor: The House That Remembers*, and her short stories have appeared in anthologies from Dark Lit Press. Her poetry has appeared in *Conceptions Southwest* and The Oklahoman Review. Along with Jamie Stewart, she is the co-editor of the Dark Lit Press anthology *The Sacrament*. Kelly lives in New Mexico. You can find her on Instagram @kellybrocklehurst.

Crozier, Bri 'Pi'

Bri 'Pi' Crozier is well known for their deep adoration of horrific fiction. A writer and illustrator with a degree in both, Bri is passionate about the natural cycle of decay and death, finding beauty in how it relates to their experiences as a queer and disabled person. When not writing or painting, Bri can be found looking for dead things in Kansas City, where they are pursuing an MFA in creative writing.

Bricrozierart.com

@ear_a_Corn Instagram & Twitter

Gómez, Cynthia

Cynthia Gómez (she/her) is a writer and researcher. She writes horror and other types of speculative fiction, set primarily in Oakland, where she makes her home. Her stories frequently contain themes of revenge, retribution, and resistance to oppression. She has stories in *The Acentos Review*, *Strange Horizons*, the collections *Antifa Splatterpunk*, *Bag of Bones: 206-Word Stories*, and the forthcoming *Split Scream* novelette series from Dread Stone Press. You can find her on Twitter at @cynthiasaysboo.

Gresham, Anne

Anne Gresham is a writer and librarian living in Northwest Arkansas with her family and a collection of tiny carnivores. Her work has appeared in Uncharted Magazine, Dark Recesses Press, Unnerving Magazine, and elsewhere. For more, visit annegresham.com or follow her on Twitter at @agresham.

Huntington, Sarah Jane

Sarah is a hospice nurse, animal lover, and the author of several short story collections, one horror novel, and two novellas. She can be found on Twitter @SarahJaneHunti1.

Mourningstarr, Violet

Evoking the beauty and power of nature, Violet Mourningstarr shines light on trauma endured by people assigned female at birth through their dark prose and verse. They're ever elusive, residing in the shadowy places often forgotten and seldom vacuumed. A staunch luddite, and happier for it, Vi cannot be found online.

Patterson, H.V.

H.V. Patterson (she/her) lives in Oklahoma and loves all things horror. She's recently published poetry and short fiction with Sliced Up Press, Shacklebound Books, *Not Deer Magazine*, Horror Tree, Dread Stone Press, and Etherea Magazine. She promotes women in horror through Dreadfulesque (@Dreadfulesque on Twitter and Instagram). Follow her on Twitter @ScaryShelley.

Rabig, Stephanie

Stephanie Rabig is the author of *On Stolen Land*, *Playing Possum*, and the *Cryptids & Cauldrons* series. When not distracting herself through books and TV shows, you can find her yelling about the state of the world on her Twitter.

Twitter—@stephrabig

Website—http://stephanierabig.weebly.com/index.html

Reynolds, Grace R.

Grace R. Reynolds is a native of the great state of New Jersey, where she was first introduced to the eerie and strange thanks to local urban legends of a devil creeping through the Pine Barrens. Since then, her curiosity with things that go bump in the night bloomed into creative expression as a dark poet, horror, and thriller fiction writer.

When Grace is not writing she can be found dreaming up macabre scenarios inspired by the mundane realities of life. Her debut collection of horror poetry *Lady of The House* was released in December 2021 by Curious Corvid Publishing.

To connect with Grace, visit www.spillinggrace.com or find her on Instagram and Twitter @spillinggrace.

Rockwell, Marsheila

Marsheila (Marcy) Rockwell (she/her) is an award-nominated tie-in writer/poet. Her work includes novels set in the Marvel Universe and in the world of Dungeons & Dragons Online, as well as numerous short stories, poems, and comic book scripts. She is a disabled pediatric cancer/ mental health awareness advocate and a reconnecting Chippewa/Métis. She lives in the Valley of the Sun with her husband, three of their five children, two rescue kitties (one from hell), and far too many books. You can find out more here: https://marsheilarockwell.com/ or follow her here: https://twitter.com/MarcyRockwell.

Sedlock, J. M.

J.M. Sedlock is a femme lesbian author in a deep love affair with all things horror and Gothic. They are usually found with their nose in a book, but they enjoy writing their own stories when they come up for air. They can be found on Twitter @jmsedlockwrites or on Instagram at jm.sedlock.

Sevens, Julie

Julie Sevens is a horror writer and an everything reader. The tentacular appendages of the universe have moved her from Ohio to Philadelphia to Berlin. Now just beyond the interstellar blast zone of Chicago, Julie lives with her husband, two sons, a doorstep spider named Lentil, and a ghost in the closet who resists naming. Find more of her nightmares at juliesevens.com.

Sylvaine, Angela

Angela Sylvaine is a self-proclaimed cheerful goth who writes horror fiction and poetry. Her debut novella, *Chopping Spree*, an homage to 1980s slashers and mall culture, is available now. Angela's short fiction has appeared in various publications and podcasts, including Dark Recesses, Places We Fear to Tread, and *The NoSleep Podcast*. Her poetry has appeared in publications including *Under Her Skin* and *Monstroddities*. You can find her online angelasylvaine.com.

Van Belle, A. J.

A. J. Van Belle is a nonbinary/transmasculine writer and scientist. Their short fiction has appeared in journals and anthologies from 2004 to the present, and their novels are represented by Lauren Bieker of FinePrint Literary Management. As a biologist, they draw on their knowledge of genetics, ecology, and statistics to inform the world-building details in their fiction. They can be found on Twitter @ ajvanbelle and at www.ajvanbelle.com.

White, Ravven

Ravven White is a queer, gothic poet and novelist. She dabbles in mystery and magic and spends most of her nights reading books or scribbling crazed stories from her pen. The founder of Curious Corvid Publishing, Ravven has a special love for the odd and the unusual and is deeply passionate about indie publishing and fair representation. Ravven lives in a castle by the sea with her husband, daughter, and their two hellhounds. You can usually sense her arrival by a curious flapping of wings. Find her here: https://linktr.ee/ curiouscorvidpublishing

Zagranis, Zack

Zack Zagranis (he/him) is a punk rock Jedi with a beard that burns brighter than the loins of Zeus. He's a boring straight guy in a family of aces, transfems, and enbys and he wouldn't have it any other way. You can follow him on Facebook, Twitter, and Instagram @zeezeeramone if you have nothing better to do.

The Editors

Bell, Nico

Nico Bell (she/her) is the author of *Beyond the Creek* and *Food Fright*. She is an award-winning author and the co-editor of a fat positive horror anthology entitled *Diet Riot: A Fatterpunk Anthology*. When she isn't reading horror books or writing, she can be found spending time with her family and two dogs. Readers can learn more about her at www.nicobellfiction.com or on Twitter, TikTok, or Instagram @nicobellfiction.

Voorhees, Roxie

Roxie Voorhees (she/he/they) is a tangled threesome of Gag Me with a Spoon, Welcome to the Darkside, and Catch Me Outside. When she isn't reading, she is writing, and when she isn't writing, she is creating something with her hands while binge-watching Buffy.

Originally from Central California, he now resides with his service dog, Bellatrix, in NE Indiana, where he refuses to use the word pop, is hella progressive, and dreams of a proper taco.

They are currently co-editing *READER BEWARE: A Fear Street Appreciation Anthology*.

Instagram: @the.book.slayer
Twitter: @theb00kslayer
Goodreads: www.goodreads.com/rvthebookslayer
Website: www.roxievoorhees.gay

Creature Publishing was founded on a passion for feminist discourse and horror's potential for social commentary and catharsis. Seeking to address the gender imbalance and lack of diversity traditionally found in the horror genre, Creature is a platform for stories which challenge the status quo. Our definition of feminist horror, broad and inclusive, expands the scope of what horror can be and who can make it.

CPSIA information can be obtained
at www.ICGtesting.com
Printed in the USA
LVHW102322011222
734454LV00006B/487